Wall Of Glory

The Princess Maura Tales
Saga of the de Magela Family

Book Three

Abigail Keam

Worker Bee Press

Worker Bee Press
P.O. Box 485
Nicholasville, KY 40340

Acknowledgements

Thanks to my editors,
Patti DeYoung and Heather McCurdy

Artwork by Karin Claesson
www.karinclaessonart.com

Book Jacket by Peter Keam
Author's photograph by Peter Keam

Also by Abigail Keam

The Josiah Reynolds Mystery Series
Death By A HoneyBee I
Death By Drowning II
Death By Bridle III
Death By Bourbon IV
Death By Lotto V
Death By Chocolate VI
Death By Haunting VII
Death By Derby VIII
Death By Design IX
Death By Malice X

The Princess Maura Epic Fantasy Tales
Wall Of Doom I
Wall Of Peril II
Wall Of Glory III
Wall Of Conquest IV
Wall Of Victory V

Last Chance For Love Series
Last Chance Motel I
Gasping For Air II
The Siren's Call III
Hard Landing IV
The Mermaid's Carol V

Audio Books
Last Chance Motel I
Gasping For Air II

Dedicated to all women who struggle
to be free from the tyranny of men.

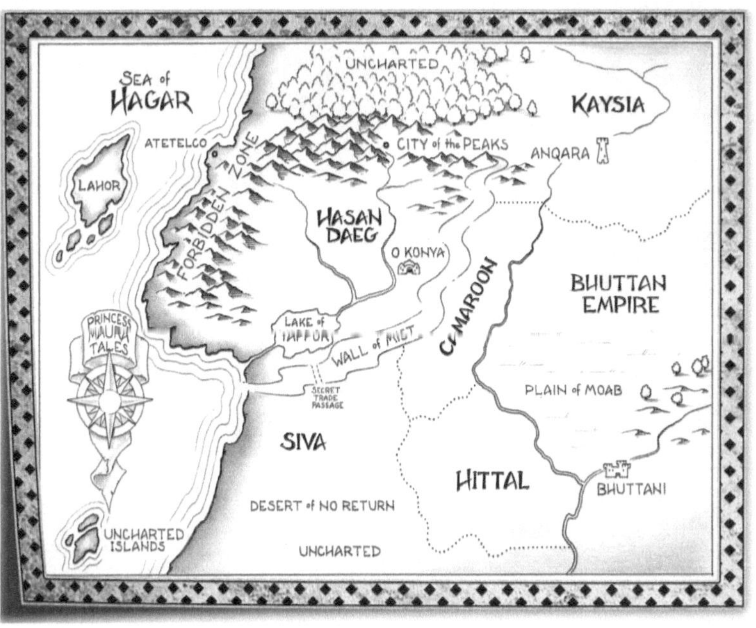

SEA of HAGAR
UNCHARTED
KAYSIA
ATETELCO
CITY of the PEAKS
ANQARA
LAHOR
FORBIDDEN ZONE
HASAN DAEG
O KONYA
BHUTTAN EMPIRE
PRINCESS MAUNA TALES
LAKE of TAPPUR
WALL of MIST
CIMAROON
PLAIN of MOAB
SIVA
SECRET TRADE PASSAGE
HITTAL
BHUTTANI
DESERT of NO RETURN
UNCHARTED ISLANDS
UNCHARTED

The Princess Maura Series Glossary

Abisola de Magela (character) – ninth queen of Hasan Daeg and mother of Princess Maura

Aga (character) – term for king of the Bhuttanians

Akela (character) – homeless Bhuttanian waif who serves KiKu and Timon

Alexanee (character) – top Bhuttanian general, illegitimate older brother of Dorak

Anqara (place) – ancient cultural and banking city located in country of Kaysia

Atetelco (place) – former capital of the Dinii located in the Forbidden Zone

Beca (character) – Princess Maura's pony

Benzar (character) – gray male hawk from secret society that protects Maura

Bes Amon Ptah (character) – Moab prince hiding under the name of Timon Ben Ibin Moab

Bhutta (character) – female deity of Bhuttanians, wife of Bhuttu

Bhuttan (place) – country ruled by Zoar and his son, Dorak

Bhuttani (place) – capital of Bhuttan

Bhuttanians (characters) – nomadic people who rose to world domination under the leadership of Zoar

Bhuttu (character) – male deity of Bhuttanians whose worship calls for the sacrifice of one's life

Bilboa (characters) – race of people with red eyes who see in the dark

Bird People (characters) – the Dinii who were Overlords of Kaseri

Black Cacodemon (character) – evil wizard of Bhuttu

Blue and gold – royal colors of the Hasan Daegians

Blue Queen (character) – nickname for Maura

Boaeps – small domesticated hopping animals

Borax (both plural and singular) – bison-like animals with sharp blades down their spines

Camaroon (place) – borders Hasan Daeg, absorbed by Bhuttanian Empire

Cappet (character) – petty thief, controls eastern part of Bhuttani

Caromate plant – provides hypnotic mist when leaves are pressed

Chaun Maaun (character) – prince of the Dinii and son of the Dinii Empress Gitar

City of the Peaks (place) – city on top of highest peak in Hasan Daeg where the Dinii live

Colla – nuts from the colla tree, brewed for teas

de Magela (characters) – name of ruling family in Hasan Daeg

Dini (character) – singular of Dinii

Dinii (characters) – ancient rulers of Kaseri, formerly called Overlords, human-like beings covered with feathers who fly

Divigi (character) – spiritual leader of the Dinii and uncle to Empress Gitar

Dorak (character) – son of Zoar, aga of the Bhuttanians

Duchy of Enos (place) – estate passed down through the family of Iasos, husband of Queen Abisola

Duke Enos (character) – father of Iasos

Dyanna (character) – princess born to Maura and Dorak

Everlynd (character) – duchess of Enos and sister of Prince Consort Iasos

Forbidden Zone (place) – former home of the Dinii, cursed by both the Dinii and Hasan Daegians

Gitar (character) – empress of the Dinii and Hasan Daegians

Gootee – duck-like animal

Great Death – name given to the practice of Hasan Daegian queens willing themselves to die

Great Mother – title of respect for older women or those in power, including queens of Hasan Daeg

Hasan Daeg (place) – peaceful agricultural country ruled by the Dinii and the de Magela family

Hasan Daegian betrothal (custom) – woman asks man permission to court by kissing man's hand; if man wishes to engage, he returns the kiss; woman gives man flowers

Hasan Daegians (characters) – peaceful agricultural people who were former slaves of the Dinii

Hetmaan (character) – Bhuttanian term for Spymaster KiKu

Hittal (place) – country conquered by Zoar, land of KiKu the Hetmaan

House of Magi (place) – ancient residence of scholars in Anqara

Iasos (character) – consort of Queen Abisola and father of Princess Maura

Iegani (character) – uncle to Empress Gitar, spiritual advisor to the Dinii, and founder of secret society that protects Princess Maura

Jezra (character) – first wife to Dorak, mother of his first child

Jon (character) – minister to Governor Petenptope of the northern Hasan Daegian state of Kinton

Kaseri (place) – name of the planet

Kaysia (place) – land in which Anqara was located

KiKu (character) – Zoar's Hetmaan, former prince of Hittal who becomes a double spy

KiKusan (character) – daughter of Kiku and concubine of Zoar

Kimtimee (character) – Queen Abisola's highest-ranking general

Kinton (place) – northern region of Hasan Daeg

Kittum (place) – country to the east of Hasan Daeg which has a treaty with Bhuttan

Knoxel (character) – magician who was mentor to Zedek

Land of the Setting Sun (place) – romantic name given to Hasan Daeg by the Bhuttanians

Lahor (place) – former island home of the Lahorians

Lahorians (characters) – originally from Lahor and ancient enemies of the Dinii

Madric (character) – KiKu's first wife

Mamora (character) – first wife of Zoar and sister of KiKu

Maura (character) – tenth ruler of Hasan Daeg, daughter of Queen Abisola and Consort Iasos

Meagan of Skujpor (character) – healer to the royal house of de Magela and member of the House of Magi

Mehmet (character) – high priestess of the House of Magi

Mekonia (character) – nature goddess of the Hasan Daegians

MeNe (character) – Yesemek's first lieutenant

Mikkotto (character) – Hasan Daegian baroness who becomes a traitor and joins with Zoar

Mingo tree – tree with large, flat limbs that is treasured for its endurance, beauty, and strength

Mother Bogazkoy/Royal Bogazkoy – intelligent, self-aware plants that have a special relationship with Hasan Daegian rulers

Nani (character) – adopted granddaughter of Lady Sari

Noabini (character) – Mehmet's assistant who becomes high priestess of the House of Magi

O Konya (place) – capital of Hasan Daeg

Onxor (character) – priest of Bhuttu

Pearl (character) – second wife of KiKu and a healer

Petenptope (character) – governor of the northern Hasan Daegian province of Kinton

Plain of Moab (place) – traditional home of nomadic people

Prosperot (character) – one of two top Bhuttanian generals, along with Alexanee

Qatou (place) – Hasan Daegian city

Rakel (character) – Lahorian woman who helps Princess Maura

Red – royal color of the Bhuttanians

Renna (character) – daughter of Riza

Riza (character) – scion from oldest noble family in Hasan Daeg

Rooshars – rare marsh flower

Rosalind (character) – first queen of Hasan Daeg

Royal Bogazkoy – plant offspring of the Mother Bogazkoy

Rubank (character) – consul to Queen Abisola and then to Queen Maura

Sari (character) – Hasan Daegian nurse to Queen Maura/Queen Abisola and grandmother of Mikkotto and Nani

Shaybar – Bhuttanian drink of boiled water or milk mixed with an equal portion of borax blood

Siddig (character) – Bhuttanian healer who helped Timon

Sinjo – rare berry made into wine that stimulates feelings of pleasure

Siva (place) – desert country south of Hasan Daeg

Sivans (characters) – merchant desert people

Sumsumitoyo (character) – family name of Mikkotto and Sari

Tarsus (character) – gray male hawk Dini who belongs to secret society that protects Maura

Tippa/Tippu (characters) – third and fourth twin wives of KiKu, artists

Tnpothar (character) – Zoar's father

Toppo (character) – red female hawk Dini, belongs to the secret society that protects Maura

Tsnsuni – ritualistic national prayer for the Hasan Daegian queen

Uultepes – mythical animals that are the symbol of Hasan Daegian royalty

Water Orbs – Lahorian mechanical devices constructed for transportation

Wise Ones (character) – title for the Lahorians

Yagomba tree – largest hardwood tree on Kaseri, has mystical powers

Yappor (place) – sacred lake of the Hasan Daegians and thought to be home of their goddess, Mekonia; home to the Lahorians

Yesemek (character) – commander-in-chief of the Dinii and wife to Iegani

Yeti (character) – red female hawk Dini, belongs to secret society that protects Maura

Yubuto (character) – sacrificed son of Mikkotto

Zedek (character) – Black Cacodemon's given name

Zoar (character) – aga (king) of the Bhuttanians

Wall Of Glory

Preface

Centuries ago, the Dinii, Overlords of the planet Kaseri, were defeated by the Lahorians, an advanced race from the sea island of Lahore.

Despondent, the Dinii retreated to Hasan Daeg, their homeland. Unable to care for their slaves, they released them from bondage while continuing to watch over them in secret.

Believing that their former masters had abandoned them, the Hasan Daegians developed into a prosperous, agricultural society, having all but forgotten their origins with the Dinii. For centuries they lived in peace, thinking their world was secure.

But to the east of Hasan Daeg, a warlike aga of Bhuttan rose—Zoar. His most burning desire was to become Overlord of the planet at any cost, thus plunging Kaseri into a wasteland.

The Lahorians, threatened by Zoar's plundering, emerged from their underwater retreat to contact their former enemies, the Dinii. Able to see into the future, the Lahorians persuaded the Dinii to establish contact with the ruling family of Hasan Daeg.

The Dinii were instructed to take the Hasan Daegian queen's only heir, Princess Maura, and train her as a Dini warrior to defeat Aga Zoar, thus allowing the Lahorians to continue their evolution into beings of pure energy.

Zoar's army finally reached the border of Hasan Daeg.

Princess Maura, commanding an army of Hasan Daegians, Anqarians, and Dinii, won the initial battle against the Bhuttanians.

In desperation, Zoar's son, Dorak, who had become the sovereign of the Bhuttanians, conjured the Black Cacodemon, an evil wizard to spin magic against the superior Hasan Daegian forces.

Unable to withstand the wizard's powerful spells, Hasan Daeg fell, and Princess Maura was taken prisoner.

Desirous of the Hasan Daeg throne and wishing the people to see his rule as legitimate, Dorak connived to marry Princess Maura while unintentionally falling in love.

Regardless, Dorak forced Maura to marry him. He also had Maura crowned Empress of Bhuttan, thus rejecting his offspring with another woman, Jezra the Anqarian.

Maura returned Dorak's love but did not trust him.

Unable to influence Dorak, Maura makes a dramatic escape and journeys to Atetelco, the ancient capital of the Dinii. There she must "mate" with the Mother Bogazkoy, a tree of mysterious abilities, so she may gain power to defeat the Black Cacodemon and set her country free of Bhuttanian dominance.

Thus our story continues with Maura fleeing O Konya.

1

Maura rushed to meet KiKu.

As a child, she had covered every inch of the city with the Dinii, memorizing every sewer hole, forgotten gate, and musty stairway in the garden city.

They planned to leave the city through an old caravan gate originally built for the Sivans that had not been used for centuries.

KiKu winced when he saw her. "Great Mother, your face is falling to your feet," he complained, watching her flesh drop to the ground.

"Just a piece here, a piece there," Maura mocked.

The alarm on KiKu's face did not vanish.

"It looks worse than it is," she said, trying to comfort him.

"You are injured! We cannot travel with you like that," KiKu insisted. He was not one to panic, but the empress' injuries were most unfortunate and ill-timed. He looked about, searching for a place to hide.

The city was being torn apart in the hunt for her. At any moment, the Bhuttanians could stumble upon them.

Maura pushed the tall man aside and mounted a Bhuttanian warhorse. "Listen, KiKu," she said. "Listen to the sound of a city being destroyed. It is all a ploy. I was meant to escape."

She donned the helmet that was hanging on the saddle horn. "How many people are going to die tonight because Dorak wants the Mother Bogazkoy? Hundreds? Thousands?" She paused, looking at the city. "Do you know what I did, KiKu? I had my women cut off the manhood from Dorak's men. I did some myself."

She pointed to her face. "This is not my blood. My blood is blue, not red. This is the blood of Bhuttanian men who stood between freedom and me. I needed a disguise to escape the palace, and those faceless men provided me one. I now know the true meaning of ruling. It is rule or be ruled. Kill or be killed."

Maura lowered the visor on her helmet and slapped the horse with the end of her reins.

The stallion whinnied and galloped off, aware that an unyielding hand controlled it.

KiKu jumped on his horse, wondering if the woman he followed had become worse than the aga he had betrayed.

2

They rode all night.

When chancing upon any Bhuttanian search parties, KiKu spoke for them, saying they had been on leave in O Konya and were now returning to their garrison in Qatou.

If any soldier questioned the blood on KiKu's partner's clothes, he would answer that O Konya was under martial law, and they had helped detain many citizens before leaving for their garrison.

Each time the bands of soldiers let them pass, not realizing that the tall Bhuttanians were the empress and Zoar's former spylord.

Before dawn, KiKu led them to a small cave on a ridge just large enough to conceal them and their mounts. Two fresh mounts waited inside with needed provisions.

Maura jumped off her horse and collapsed on a bedroll that KiKu provided her. She was exhausted both physically and mentally.

KiKu handed Maura hardtack and a cup of water. "There will be no fire tonight," KiKu apologized. "Sorry about the rations, but I had only a few hours to arrange for this little escape of yours."

Maura grunted in agreement. "It is good that your cohorts can move so quickly and easily." She pondered for a moment.

"Getting these warhorses was no small task. How many Bhuttanians still work for you, KiKu?"

KiKu blinked while leaning against a rock munching on some hardtack. "The beauty of my system, Great Mother, is that if caught, you will never have any information to divulge to Dorak that could threaten my loyal followers."

She chortled. "In other words the less I know, the better."

"Correct, Great Mother."

"What do you get out of this if I win?"

"Your mother promised me my kingdom. I wish to gather my people if there are any left."

"My mother's wish is now my command, KiKu. I swear to you that if we prevail, you will have your kingdom."

"Upon your oath as Great Mother?"

"Upon my oath as Empress Maura de Magela."

"Then indeed we shall prevail." KiKu swallowed some water and rested his head on his chest.

Thinking KiKu had fallen asleep, Maura got up to care for the horses.

KiKu stuck his foot out and shook his head while still resting his closed eyes. "I will see to the horses in a moment, Great Mother. You must sleep."

Maura gratefully returned to her bedroll and was dreaming before her head came to rest.

3

Maura awoke.

She found KiKu squatting before the entrance of the cave surveying the valley below. "Any sign of trouble?" she asked, rubbing her sore muscles.

KiKu shook his head slightly. "Search parties were down in the valley. They have left to go on to Qatou, I suppose." He looked at Maura intently. "Your face doesn't look any better," he commented.

She felt her features with her hands, as there was no mirror. "Some of the cuts are starting to get infected," she said. "I feel feverish."

"Can you do anything about it?" KiKu asked.

Maura shrugged her shoulders. "I guess I could heal myself before we leave tonight."

"Great Mother, may I suggest that if you can do so, you do it now. We may have to flee at any moment, and it would not do to have a sick woman on my hands."

Maura rubbed her face and did not answer KiKu.

"Great Mother, I know you are feeling sad about the death of Lady Sari, but being a ruler sometimes involves knowing when not to put your servants in needless danger."

Maura flinched at the mention of Sari and began to weep silently. "You know about Sari?"

"Before you came to the wall, one of my contacts made a brief visit. She told me that an imposter posing as you had committed suicide rather than be taken. I guessed it was Lady Sari."

"And my guards?"

"It is correct that you cry for them. It shows you still have a heart, and you honor them with your tears."

"If I had a heart, I would not have let them die."

"What else was to be done? You had to flee the city, and they willingly gave their lives to ensure that you could. They knew what they were doing. It is our way."

Maura gave KiKu a long, hard look. "Who?"

"Those who serve, Great Mother. We know our lives are expendable, and we accept our lot in life." His expression was one of acceptance and regret.

Maura left KiKu with his memories and moved to the back of the cave where she relieved herself. When finished, she perched upon a rock in the cave and began healing her face.

KiKu did not watch but gazed upon the valley, watching a hawk soar in the sky. If he could have escaped being spotted, KiKu would have contacted the hawk to take a message to the Dinii, but it was too much of a risk to call out.

An hour later, Maura jumped down from the rock and washed her face from a small tin of water. "How do I look?" she asked KiKu.

He studied her face, looking for marks or cuts. "You look like a young woman again, but you have the blue face of a de Magela."

KiKu walked to the opposite side of her, again studying her face. "I have heard of your regenerative powers, but this is the first time I have witnessed them for myself. It is amazing. Have you still the fever?"

"See for yourself."

KiKu cautiously extended his hand and touched her brow. "Dry and cool. No fever," he pronounced happily. "We will be able to travel tonight."

Maura nodded in agreement. "Where do we go from here?"

"We will travel south into Siva. There we will pose as a merchant with his obedient and humble wife."

Maura teased, "Are you going to pose as the wife?"

KiKu smiled a toothy grin.

For the first time, Maura noticed that KiKu was a good-looking man and not as old as she had believed. She wondered if he had a wife stashed away somewhere. "Why don't we head north to the City of the Peaks?"

KiKu's smile vanished.

Alarmed, Maura grabbed his arm. "Why do you look like that? What has happened?"

KiKu bowed his head. He did not want to see her face as he told her. "The City of the Peaks is no more. Burned out."

Maura cried, "How? The city is impregnable!"

"Magic," was KiKu's reply.

"The Black Cacodemon!" Maura spat on the ground. Her face contorted as though she were struggling to find the right words. "What of the royal family—Empress Gitar and her children?" she asked quietly.

"I don't know. I suppose some got out."

"Why?" Maura felt as though someone had gutted her with a knife.

KiKu rubbed his unshaven face. "Dorak did not want the Dinii to help you if you fled. He put them on the run. I think you are right in that this is a trick, too. Soldiers should have been swarming over that west wall. We did not see any until the road patrols. Easy enough to fool them. I think the hitch in their plans was that your disguise was too good. You threw them off, and now they've got to find you."

"To follow us!"

"Correct," KiKu said. His respect for the girl had increased. She was not stupid and, judging from her masquerade, was resourceful as well as ruthless. He had not recognized her at all when she first approached, and he was a master of disguises. "Dorak wants the Mother Bogazkoy."

"She will not accept him. He is not suitable for her purposes."

"Perhaps he doesn't know that or he doesn't believe it. Perhaps the Black Cacodemon has promised him the mating will work."

"Perhaps, perhaps. I need facts. I need to know who remains of the Dinii. I need to know where my western army is. You are supposed to be my spylord. Tell me something of value," she prodded in frustration.

"No one has seen the Dinii since the attack. We do not know where they have gone. They could have left the country."

"No," challenged Maura. "Chaun Maaun would never have left me. Never!"

"Chaun Maaun could be no longer, and you did marry someone else."

Maura's face drained of color. She looked almost

pale. "I was forced into marriage!"

KiKu gave a look that challenged the veracity of this last statement.

Maura buried her face in her warhorse's long mane, weeping. "That's a lie. I wanted to marry Dorak." Tears ran down her cheeks as shame illuminated her face.

The spy was moved to pity her. "We cannot help with whom we fall in love."

"But I loved Chaun Maaun and hated Dorak, at least in the beginning."

"Who knows the will of the heart? It can love many people in many ways. It can also hate and love at the same time. Zoar loved my sister, but he let her die in a hunting accident. Dorak both loved and hated his father, and yet he murdered him."

Maura wiped her tears away. "Dorak killed Zoar?"

KiKu nodded solemnly.

The horse on which Maura leaned shifted and nuzzled her arm with his nose. "I don't know why, but that news makes me feel better."

"Misery abides company?"

"It explains Dorak's suffering." Maura scratched behind the ears of the contented horse. "I am content that he suffers as I do."

"I think Dorak suffers a great deal. If he had been born with better parents, such as mine, he would have been a great man."

"Like you?"

KiKu ignored her sarcasm. "Dorak has the seeds of greatness within him, but with Zoar as his father, he didn't stand a chance to grow without being twisted in some fashion. Dorak was right to kill him."

"Who am I to judge Dorak when I allowed my beloved Sari to be killed?"

"You still do not realize."

"What?"

"Dorak is not the man to fear, nor the Black Cacodemon. It is Alexanee who must be watched."

"Why him?"

"Dorak will make a mistake that will cost him his life because he is impetuous." KiKu picked up some pebbles and flipped them back and forth between his fingers. "Like Dorak, the Black Cacodemon must be dealt with, but he is not invincible. His fatal defect is his ambition. Sooner or later, a spell will backfire, or Dorak will tire of him and do the bastard in with one thrust of a sword. They are capable but flawed men who will perish from their own miscalculations."

KiKu put a pebble in his mouth and began to suck on it. "Alexanee is different," he continued after he spat out the small stone. "He has no weaknesses. He does not gamble. He stays away from women. He is not a religious fanatic. Alexanee is highly intelligent, a brilliant strategist, even better than Zoar in his heyday. He is a man of moderation, both spiritually and emotionally."

Maura was intrigued by KiKu's analysis of Alexanee. She had never given him much thought. "It does not matter what attributes Alexanee has. He can never be aga."

"You are wrong, Great Mother. Only three people stand between Alexanee and his gaining control of the Bhuttanian Empire. Dorak, Jezra's son, and you."

KiKu lowered his voice. "Alexanee is Zoar's first child, born on the wrong side of the blanket you might say. His mother was a Bhuttanian noblewoman who was much older than Zoar. The details of Alexanee's birth remained quiet, but when his mother died, Zoar brought Alexanee to court to serve as an officer in his army. Since Alexanee's parentage was not known, Zoar spared his life when killing the rest of his sons in favor of Dorak."

"Does he know?"

"Neither Dorak nor Alexanee know. I became privy to this information when Zoar and I were watching Alexanee train once. Zoar said, 'There goes the best one of the lot, and I can't acknowledge him.'"

"And then you did some digging on your own?"

"Yes."

Maura remained silent while stroking the horse.

KiKu realized she did not wish to talk further. The hetmaan spent the remainder of the day resting near the mouth of the cave, though deep sleep eluded him. Noticing that he could no longer see the sun, KiKu looked outside. It was growing dark, and soon it would be safe for them to leave. He saddled the horses.

Maura, who had been resting quietly on her bedroll, fell into step with KiKu to help with the horses and gather their gear. When finished, KiKu told the young empress to wait outside with their new mounts.

The young queen was sad for she knew the fate of the two still-exhausted horses they had ridden from O Konya.

KiKu could not let them roam loose as their discovery would give away the direction of their escape.

Maura took the reins of the fresh mounts and walked a bit from the cave. She held her breath waiting for a panicked whinny or scream but heard nothing.

KiKu soon joined her, sheathing his knife. Taking his reins and a hank of mane, the lithe man pulled himself upon the warhorse.

"I have killed many a man, but I can't abide hurting an animal." He put on his helmet. "Don't you think that strange?" Without waiting for an answer, he kicked his horse and started down the mountain.

Maura followed behind, ever alert for trouble.

They had traveled several miles when Maura heard a rustling in a nearby tree and looked up, her hand upon her sword.

Yeti sat upon a limb calmly eating a hedgepear. She looked happily at Maura and waved, "Greetings, Great Mother. I have been sent to fetch you!"

4

Yeti took another bite.

"Yeti!" exclaimed Maura, turning her horse around. She jumped down and tied the horse securely to a low branch.

Yeti threw away her pear and glided down gracefully. Standing in the moonlight, she towered over Maura. She fluttered her massive wings in greeting and smiled a wide, sloppy grin.

The horse shied nervously, but Yeti spoke to it soothingly and patted its roan neck.

The stallion settled down and began munching on grass.

Maura asked excitedly, "How did you find me?" She grabbed Yeti's hand and squeezed it with genuine affection.

"We heard that you had escaped. Iegani sent us out

to find you and take you to the Forbidden Zone."

"I am ready now."

Yeti held up her hand. "You cannot travel with me. It is too dangerous. I can only guide you."

"I don't understand," Maura said, her heart sinking.

"It is the Black Cacodemon," said KiKu, steadying his horse.

"Greetings, Hetmaan of Queen Maura," Yeti said, her wings fluttering.

KiKu noticed the Dini did not refer to Maura as empress.

"You know his face?" asked Maura incredulously. "The identity of the hetmaan should be known only to a certain few."

"It is the first time I have seen him, but the Dinii know of the lord who worked as a double agent for Queen Abisola. Otherwise, how could I have rendezvoused with you in the meadow for our last meeting? He sends messages to us via the gootee." Yeti bowed in respect. "A master of disguises. I almost mistook you both for Bhuttanian soldiers and was going to kill you, but then I saw you were not Bhuttanian."

KiKu raised his eyebrows. "How is that?"

"Bhuttanians ride with their knees higher and heels turned downward. You ride with your feet level."

Yeti turned toward Maura. "You ride well, but you

look uncomfortable, as though you are unfamiliar with handling such a big animal. Nothing I could see directly. Just what I felt when I saw you."

"Lady, you are most observant. I could use someone like you. Would you like to be a spy?" KiKu teased.

Yeti laughed easily. "I don't think I could easily blend in with the common folk."

KiKu jumped down off his horse and joined Yeti and Maura. He handed Yeti a waterskin from which she drank sparingly, due more to good manners than lack of thirst.

"I heard you say that you were sent here to fetch the empress," KiKu commented.

Yeti handed the waterskin back to him and nodded. "You are headed toward the border of Siva. There are bounty hunters and bandits waiting for you to cross."

KiKu whistled. This was a mighty blow to his plans. "Is there a reward?"

"Yes, but not from the Royal House of the Aga. It is offered by Baroness Mikkotto. She has put up the money."

"Mikkotto!" Maura ranted. "That murderous bitch."

Yeti, undisturbed by Maura's ire, continued, "The baroness has resettled on her estates with impunity. Other than answering to Dorak, she fears no one and is a law unto herself. Her estate is guarded by Hasan

Daegians loyal to her cause and Bhuttanians who serve as mercenaries."

Maura seemed stunned and wove a bit on her feet as though she were about to faint. She rubbed her forehead. "That would mean Dorak gave her permission to resettle. It means my parents' death by Mikkotto's plot was a ruse. He was going to kill them anyway, and he used her as a tool."

"It would seem so," replied Yeti, thinking kindly of Abisola and Iasos. They had been worthy rulers, and she was sorry they were gone.

Maura cast a wicked eye upon KiKu. "Did you know of this?"

KiKu shook his head and looked questioningly at Yeti. "None of my sources have mentioned Mikkotto since last spring. I find this information surprising."

Maura slapped KiKu hard across the face, almost knocking him off his feet. "You had better not be lying to me. If you fail me again, I will kill you."

KiKu's face remained hard and impassive, but it was evident that he was struggling to control himself. He took off his corselet of chain mail and dropped it on the ground, then put his hand on his sword.

Yeti stepped forward, but Maura grabbed her arm.

KiKu unsheathed his sword and presented its hilt to Maura.

She took it.

"I have offended thee. I am dishonored. Take my life so that I may die with honor, or permit me to die by my hand," he begged.

"I will neither kill you nor grant you permission to die by suicide," said Maura coldly. "You have treated me like a child since we met. I will forgive you since I have indeed acted as a child who could not see beyond her nose. But now I am truly the Ruling Lady of Hasan Daeg. Do you know why?"

Maura tapped on her chest as she spoke. "Because in here, there is no more a child, only a queen who needs your help getting to the Mother Bogazkoy so she may fulfill her destiny." She pointed the sword to the ground. "Pledge your allegiance to me."

KiKu fell to his knees, his face red with shame that he had failed his sovereign. He prostrated himself before Maura. "I pledge with my life and honor that I will live to obey you in all things and to serve the House of de Magela."

Maura asked, "Upon your life?"

"Upon my life!"

"Rise then and serve me well. We will never discuss this again."

KiKu rose from the ground and dusted off his clothes. He seemed genuinely chastised.

Yeti wondered if she would eventually have to kill him to protect Maura. It would be a pity as KiKu was such a valuable resource.

She sauntered over to a kokobo tree and pulled a small pouch from a knothole, handing it to Maura. "You are not to go by land to Siva. You are to go to the Sacred Lake of Yappor. There the Lahorians will take care of you."

"The Lahorians again," scoffed Maura, opening the pouch. She handed the contents to KiKu who held them up to the moonlight so all could see.

Yeti waved him away. "I can see in the dark without light," she said.

Inside the pouch was a map drawn on leather with berry juice. Maura was surprised and looked at Yeti. "Did you do this?"

Yeti smiled. "I can also read and write. Empress Gitar decided everyone needed to read, so we all learned. Badly at first, but better as time goes on."

She fingered the outlines on the map. "Here is an old hunter's trail that you will take to the Sacred Lake. From there the Lahorians will transport you and KiKu to the Forbidden Zone."

The hairs on the back of Maura's neck stood up at the mention of the Forbidden Zone, a place not visited by any Hasan Daegian since prohibited by Mekonia, their nature goddess.

"Why can't you fly the empress to the lake?" asked KiKu.

"Is empress your title now?" asked Yeti.

Maura lowered her eyes. "There is only one empress, and she is Gitar."

"Yes, that is what she thinks. She would want me to remind you," Yeti replied.

Peering at the map, KiKu asked again, "Why can't you transport her to the lake?"

Yeti lowered her head to study the bald man. "Because you will have a better chance of making it if you remain disguised as Bhuttanians. With me, there is too great a risk that we would be shot out of the sky. The Bhuttanians have been ordered to shoot anything larger than an eagle flying. I only travel easily when the sky is pitch black. There is a full moon tonight. We would make an easy target."

"Makes sense," said KiKu as he folded the map. He seemed to have forgotten the unsettling reprimand he had received only moments before.

"What of Gitar and Chaun Maaun?" asked Maura, her heart slowing down to take the shock of any bad news.

"I cannot tell you where they are, but they are alive," Yeti replied, her face lined with sadness. "Empress

Gitar has aged with grief. All her daughters were killed when the Black Cacodemon destroyed the city."

Maura groaned.

"Chaun Maaun lives. He never leaves his mother's side." Yeti handed the pouch to KiKu, who placed the map carefully inside his tunic. "He wants to see you, Maura."

Maura's eyes widened with apprehension. "Where?"

"He would not say. He wanted me only to tell you that he will see you but at his discretion."

Maura's heart raced as her eyes took on a strange light.

Yeti placed her hand on Maura's shoulder.

"Don't expect too much, little sparrow. He has changed and is not the same Chaun Maaun that you knew before. It has been terrible for him. He lives now only to hate the Bhuttanians. He is consumed with it."

"Does he wish to harm our queen?" KiKu asked, wondering how he was going to subdue a Dini. Without waiting for an answer, KiKu pleaded with Maura, "You must not see him."

Maura shamelessly brushed a tear from her cheek. "Tell Chaun Maaun I will see him on his conditions."

"You must not!" KiKu reiterated. "If he is that angry, he might try to kill you." KiKu looked at Yeti for support.

None was forthcoming.

"I will give him the satisfaction of calling me a traitor."

KiKu said, "What if he tries to kill you? Not even you can fight a Dini!"

Maura whispered, "Do you think that is the worst thing he can do to me?"

Yeti grunted with approval.

KiKu was desperate. "Yeti, help me. Persuade her not to see Prince Chaun Maaun."

Yeti shrugged her shoulders. "Chaun Maaun was her betrothed. His love was as pure as the water in the Sacred Lake of Yappor. She betrayed him for a human who was a murderer and butcher of both Hasan Daegians and Dinii. Now he wants satisfaction. It is the Dinii way. Maura was raised with the Dinii. She will follow our customs in this matter."

"You knew about us?" asked Maura.

"Little sparrow, everyone knew. The young hide their love not well at all." Yeti looked at the night sky. "You must hurry now. Every minute counts. I will follow you when I can. If anyone comes after you, I will kill them. Remember—take the short cut to the Sacred Lake of Yappor."

"What happens once we get there?" asked KiKu.

Stand at the edge of the lake. "The Lahorians are

waiting for you and keeping watch. Once you arrive, they will transport you to the Forbidden Zone. You must do as they say."

"Can they be trusted?"

Yeti smiled. "As much as an old enemy can be. Their survival depends upon you at the moment. They will keep you safe enough."

Maura hugged Yeti warmly, inhaling her musky scent.

Yeti rested her chin on the top of Maura's head and brought her wings around to encircle them. "You smell like a barn, Yeti," whispered Maura.

"That is what you have always said, little sparrow," cooed Yeti, embracing Maura with her powerful wings. Yeti gave her one last tight squeeze before retracting her wings. "You must go now. Be careful." Yeti cuffed Maura under the chin.

"Chaun Maaun?"

"I will tell him that you will meet with him. Now go!"

Maura jumped onto her horse and sped off, following KiKu.

Yeti watched them until they disappeared deep into the forest and then flew back to her hiding place in the tree.

Tarsus handed her another hedgepear. "She looks

good for having gone through so much."

"The young always recover fast."

"That was a very inventive lie about Mikkotto and Dorak," Tarsus commented.

"It is Iegani's doing, not mine. It's a dirty business, but I see no benefit for lying to Maura." Yeti threw the hedgepear away in disgust.

"Will Iegani let her see Chaun Maaun?"

Yeti wiped her mouth with her forearm. "Not even Iegani can control the prince. Chaun Maaun will have his way eventually."

Tarsus grunted and leaned back against a limb, quickly falling asleep.

Yeti watched the moon. She felt deeply for the woman she had held as a baby and guarded. She remembered the times she had picked up the child who gurgled and laughed as she pulled on Yeti's feathers. Yeti felt a stirring in her heart that she did not quite understand but accepted.

She loved the girl and felt Iegani was wrong to deceive her. Nothing good would come of it. Sooner or later, it would catch up with him. Hopefully, Yeti would be far away when that happened.

5

KiKu and Maura rode hard.

Just as they thought they were safe, they ran into a patrol coming off the plains.

The leader, a rough looking Bhuttanian, did not believe KiKu's story about rejoining his unit after a leave in O Konya. He ordered KiKu and Maura off their horses.

Just as he was going to have his men take out their weapons, Maura struck his horse with her hunting knife and gutted it. The warhorse screamed as it staggered and fell, crushing the patrol leader underneath.

Maura jumped at another horse that sidestepped out of her reach.

The rider swung his baton, striking Maura on the side of her head, crushing the side of her helmet.

Blood swam into her eyes. Years of training came to

the forefront, and Maura countered a deathblow aimed at her neck.

Maura scurried under the trained horse that snorted with anger and fright, striking at her with sturdy legs and hooves. Pulling off her helmet, she reached up and swung her sword, cutting the soldier's leg and stirrup off at the ankle.

The soldier shrieked with pain, falling to the ground in shock.

Maura made quick work of him.

KiKu was surrounded by three angry soldiers who did their best to punch him. Like a butterfly, he flitted out of their range, countering their blows with savage leg kicks. His fight was entirely defensive as he had left his sword in the chest of a nameless opponent and couldn't pull it out in time to defend against his three new adversaries. Using his peripheral vision, KiKu scanned for Maura and caught a blur moving beneath a horse. He heard someone scream but couldn't identify the source. He inwardly prayed that Maura would come to his rescue as he was getting tired, and one of the three men would soon breach his defensive strategy.

Unexpectedly, the man on his left grunted and threw up his hands, dropping his sword. He fell backwards with a heavy thud revealing Maura standing behind him.

She immediately turned her attention to the dead

man's comrade who charged at her in a fury.

Maura smiled coolly at him.

The lifeless smile gave the rushing man pause, and he veered off at the last moment.

Unfortunately for him, his path was not wide enough.

Maura struck out with her sword and caught him deep in the side.

The man grabbed his side and cried out, stumbling to the ground. She leaned over him and finished him with a jab to the neck.

KiKu pummeled his last opponent with lightning-quick blows with his fists and legs. KiKu thought beating a man to death took an awfully long time for both the victor and the soon-to-be-dead man. He knocked the man unconscious and mercifully broke the man's neck. KiKu fell to the ground, breathing heavily. He looked about him and saw the bloody remains of five men and two horses.

The other horses, including their own, had run off but he could hear them snorting nearby. They were trained not to go far.

Maura walked toward KiKu and stood over him peering down. "You are getting too old for this," she said reproachfully.

KiKu watched her calmly wipe her sword clean on

the grass. "I have many good years ahead of me. You have the strength of the Bogazkoy that gives you an unfair advantage."

"That unfair advantage just saved your life."

"I'm not complaining," said KiKu, extending his hand.

Maura reached down and pulled him up.

They both looked at the cooling corpses on the ground.

"We need to hide them."

"We don't have time. Besides, Yeti will come along and take care of this," Maura said.

KiKu wiped the sweat from his forehead. "I don't know. Another patrol could come along and find them."

Maura grew impatient. "We don't have time to dispose of five men and two huge horses. Let us be off!"

She strode with purpose to where she heard the horses grazing and quickly caught the reins of one. She mounted and caught the reins of the other horses. "We will bring them along with us," she said, starting off.

KiKu jumped on one of the horses, secretly glad he would not have to kill any more animals. He rummaged through its saddlebags and found rolled bread and meat paste. He caught up with Maura and shared his bounty with her. They both tore ravenously at the bread, which tasted like a bland pancake, but were grateful for any food.

The young empress rode through the night as though propelled by some deep and unfathomable force.

Occasionally, KiKu caught her lips moving silently as though she were communicating with someone or something. Her face had taken on a darker pallor.

The hetmaan worried about the warhorses. Even though they had been bred for endurance, KiKu knew they were starting to tire.

Every hour, he and Maura would switch mounts while still moving. He cautioned her that they were wearing out the horses, but she paid KiKu no heed and rode on.

At dawn, they rested for only an hour or so.

Maura sensed they were near the Sacred Lake of Yappor. As a child, Iegani and Yeti had brought her to the lake's placid shores and sat with her while Iegani instilled in her the potential of her destiny. He had only mentioned the Lahorians once, a mystical race of people of supreme intellect who lived beneath the lake and would contact her as needed. Over the years she had forgotten the Lahorians as Iegani had told her many parables. It seemed that this was one story she should have remembered. Try as she might, Maura could not remember what Iegani had said to her.

Now Maura felt a burning desire to reach the lake as soon as possible. Her throat was parched. She was constantly sipping from her waterskin, ignoring KiKu's pleas to quit drinking and to slow her horse down. She sensed her name called over and over again.

Watching KiKu out of the corner of her eye, she knew he had heard nothing. She answered with her mind, "I am coming! I am coming!" urging her tired mount forward.

They pounded into a clearing with a brook running through it.

Maura stopped her horse and dismounted, guiding her horse and several others to water.

KiKu remained mounted and studied their surroundings. He thought the clearing was an unnatural manifestation in the middle of the forest.

Suddenly, Yeti swooped down, causing the horses to bolt.

KiKu cursed as he lunged forward trying to catch the reins of the horses. "I'll be back," he called as he galloped after the fleeing horses.

The fact that Maura trusted Yeti was no reason he should trust the Dini. He thought her sudden appearance somehow staged as if to intentionally frighten the horses. He pulled his horse to a stop and turned it around, riding back to the clearing.

Both Yeti and Maura were gone.

6

Yeti set Maura down.

The yagomba tree limb was so broad several people could walk abreast comfortably on it. At the joint where the limb sprang from the trunk of the tree stood Chaun Maaun.

Chaun Maaun nodded to Yeti, and she flew off, leaving Maura alone with him.

Maura was startled at the sight of Chaun Maaun standing in the dark crook of the tree. Forgotten feelings rushed back to claim her heart. She started toward him, but he held out his hand, staving her off.

"Chaun Maaun," she whispered feverishly.

Chaun Maaun stepped out of the shadow of the tree, allowing Maura to view him closely.

She recoiled without thinking.

The Dini prince scowled. "What's the matter,

Maura? You don't like the way I look now?" he asked, venom dripping from his words. "The night of the invasion when we were supposed to leave in peace there was a lone arrow in the sky. Isn't it pretty?"

He was wearing a large patch that covered his left eye as well as part of his cheek. He turned the left side of his face toward her and pointed. "This is what your husband did to me!" He pulled off the leather patch, exposing his face. Chaun Maaun's left eye was gone, and a deep scar was carved in his cheek.

Maura whimpered, "Oh, no!" and reached out to touch him.

Chaun Maaun retreated out of Maura's reach.

Regret and longing squeezed Maura's heart. She fell to her knees and put her head in her hands, weeping. Maura reeled from the heartache that her beloved Chaun Maaun spurned her—even hated her!

"Do you think your tears will save you?" asked Chaun Maaun, sneering. His one good eye swam with tears also, but he blinked them back. He would not give her the satisfaction of seeing the pain he had suffered due to her. His voice took on an icy tone. "I want to know why!"

"Why what?" asked Maura, looking up at him. Her face was streaked with salty tears, and her nose was dark blue and swollen.

"Why did you marry him?"

"It was a challenge of combat. If I won, the Bhuttanians would leave Hasan Daeg. If he won, I would have to marry him."

"And you lost?"

Maura nodded. She looked pleadingly at him. "Please understand, Chaun Maaun. I never stopped loving you." Her face contorted in agony. "I was alone. My parents were dead. I did the best I could. I thought you were safe in the City of the Peaks. I thought he was honoring the peace."

"Dorak and that corrupt sorcerer of his destroyed it, Maura. You wouldn't even recognize it now." Chaun Maaun drifted off, thinking of that terrible day. "We truly live like animals now. Always on the run. Without proper food, without comfort. Dorak has scared off all the game. We are slowly starving to death."

Maura got to her feet and wiped her face with a sleeve. She bravely stepped toward Chaun Maaun. She knew that he could strike her dead or throw her off the tree limb, causing her to break her neck in the fall. "Please believe me. I did not know this was occurring. Dorak had me watched night and day. I had access to only a few advisors who were as blind as I. If I stepped out of bounds, he rounded up my people and tortured them."

Maura stepped closer to him. She could feel his breath and smell his woodsy smell. "You are not the only one who suffered. Please, Chaun Maaun, I can't bear this! Let us forgive one another for events over which we had no control." She embraced him, resting her head on his chest. She clung to him as if her life and sanity depended on it.

Chaun Maaun relaxed. He took a deep breath. He smelled her feminine scent, and it brought back memories of loving and being loved. His jealous rage subsided as he relived his life before the war when Maura was his.

Maura looked older now, and her eyes had taken on a hard, bitter look. There was nothing soft about them except for the few times she had looked at him, pleading with him to understand.

He understood all too well. Much of his rage was at himself for not being able to save Maura. He should have defied Dorak that night in the palace and taken her with him.

He knew that he could have grabbed her before Dorak stopped him, but Chaun Maaun had been afraid for Maura. It seemed too great a risk at the time. Now he bitterly regretted his decision. If he had taken her out of the city that night, Maura could have joined her western army and resisted Dorak.

No, that would not have been the outcome.

Chaun Maaun winced at the memory of that night. If he had flown with her out of the city, Maura would have died, as he would have dropped her when the lone arrow sliced through his eye.

Chaun Maaun shook his head. He bent down and kissed the crown of her head. No, he did the right thing by leaving her with Dorak!

Maura responded to his kiss by embracing him tighter and melting into his arms.

"What will you do now?" he asked.

"I go to join Iegani in the Forbidden Zone."

"You are going to be with the Mother Bogazkoy?"

"Yes, I think she is hidden in the Forbidden Zone near the sea."

"And if you survive, will you come back to me?" Chaun Maaun's face was warm and tender.

Maura bowed her head and pulled away from him.

Chaun Maaun felt as though he had been struck in the face. "You will not come back to me," he said with finality.

"Things are different now. We are not the same people," Maura said, her voice low and husky.

"Once the Bhuttanians are gone, we can forget."

Maura shook her head slowly. "I am their ruler now. I cannot desert them."

"You can't be serious." Chaun Maaun grabbed Maura's shoulders.

She tried not to flinch at the pain.

"Do you think Dorak intended you to be his empress? He wanted to find out the secret of the Mother Bogazkoy. He used you. If he ever discovers it, you will be as good as dead."

"No!"

"What is this!" exclaimed Chaun Maaun. He picked Maura up into the air until she was face to face with him. "You dare to defend Dorak!" He shook her hard.

Maura's teeth rattled.

"Do you have feelings for him? Do you? Damn you," he hissed. "I ought to kill you."

"Sire, I am asking you to put her down. NOW!" demanded Yeti, standing behind Maura.

Chaun Maaun's good eye was wide with rage. "She betrayed me! She betrayed our love!" he bellowed.

"No, my lord, Maura betrayed no one. If you don't put her down, I will have to disable you. I brought her to you as you commanded; now I must take her away. Iegani is waiting."

Chaun Maaun laughed like a crazy man. He swung her over the limb.

Maura was filled with terror as she looked down. She was a hundred feet in the air. Even with her recuperative powers, she wouldn't be able to survive the fall without massive injuries.

"My Prince and Lord, listen to me. I am bound by a sacred oath to protect Maura. I will kill you if I have to," cautioned Yeti, watching his every move.

She knew Tarsus waited below to catch Maura if she was, indeed, thrown over.

The agonized Chaun Maaun placed Maura back on the limb.

Maura fell into a crumpled heap and looked up at his towering figure. "I am everything you think I am."

"I don't want to hear this."

"No, listen to me so you can purge me from your heart. I have become a different woman."

Chaun Maaun shook his head in disbelief.

"It is true. I went to Dorak willingly," Maura shared.

Chaun Maaun trembled.

"I don't know why. He was never like you. I don't understand my feelings, but I do love him in some strange way."

"NO MORE!" Chaun Maaun roared. He fell beside her, a broken husk, and sobbed openly. "He must die. You understand that, don't you?"

Maura nodded her head.

"Then you can come back to me."

"We can never be."

"Why?"

"I will never heal from this terrible thing that has been thrust upon me. I could never be a true mate to you. After this war is over, you must marry from your own people. This is best for both our races. We can't think of ourselves anymore."

"You would still think of him?"

Maura said nothing and looked away.

"So you love him more."

"I love you deeply, but I am married to him. If things were different, I would want to be with you."

"I could make you forget him."

"That is impossible."

"Give me a chance."

"No, it is the principle. It is everything I stand for."

"Is principle more important than your love for me?"

"My duty to my people is more important than my love for you. And so it should be with you. But, yes, I love him more."

Chaun Maaun pushed off his feet. "Then have your principle and your love of Dorak. From this moment forward, I am your enemy. Do you understand?"

"Remember your oath to me."

"I renounce it."

"I have a reprieve until the Bhuttanians are defeated?"

"Then I will kill you."

"You can try." Maura squared back her shoulders.

Chaun Maaun took one final look at his lost love and flew off the yagomba limb, his heart breaking, never to be mended again.

7

Yeti quickly moved to Maura.

"That was a bold strategy you played. I thought Chaun Maaun was going to drop you for sure."

Maura placed her hand on the black armor protecting her belly. "Now that he has spared me, I have to stay alive until after my baby is born. She must be next in line to the throne of Bhuttan."

"What!"

Maura sorrowfully watched Chaun Maaun disappear into the sky. She replied softly, "I am carrying Dorak's child."

8

Yeti placed Maura down.

Benzar waited patiently on the shore of the Sacred Lake of Yappor with KiKu, who looked a little green around the gills.

KiKu smiled with relief when he spied Maura and rushed to her side.

"Are you all right?" he asked. He didn't even wait for an answer. "This thing," he said, pointing to Benzar who regarded KiKu with cool disdain, "swooped out of the sky and pulled me right off my horse."

Maura smiled weakly at Benzar.

Benzar acknowledged her by bowing very low. "It is good to see you again, Queen of the Hasan Daegians."

"Thank you, Benzar. It is good to see my old companion." She always thought it odd that Benzar was formal with her even though he had changed her diapers as a baby.

She turned to KiKu. "I'm fine. We may continue the journey. But what about the horses?"

"We are taking care of the horses. They will be put to good use," Yeti replied.

Maura understood Yeti's meaning. The horses were to be eaten by the Dinii.

Knowing KiKu was fond of horses, she wished to divert attention away from them. "This place looks vaguely familiar," she said.

"Should we be out in the open like this?" KiKu questioned.

Yeti took a quick look around the lake. "Dorak has diverted all his extra soldiers to the ruins of the City of the Peaks." She directed her comments to Maura. "He rightly assumed that you did not know the city was destroyed and would go there first. We have left suitable tracks for him to follow."

"The Black Cacodemon will not be fooled long by such tricks. He will use his magic to find me."

Yeti replied, "So far he has used his magic to track the Dinii only. We have spread what remains of us along the western portion of Hasan Daeg. With each little group, a Hasan Daegian woman has been placed to confuse him. I would say we have done a good job keeping him busy looking for you. He is not searching for two renegade Bhuttanian soldiers."

"Well done," commented KiKu. "I could not have succeeded better myself."

Yeti bowed to KiKu, seemingly pleased. She loved praise. It was her one vice.

"What now?" asked Maura, feeling tired.

"We will wait until the Lahorians come," replied Yeti, looking at the crystal clear water.

KiKu followed her gaze upon the vast lake. "When will that be?"

"Whenever they are ready," Maura said.

KiKu suggested, "Perhaps they do not know we are here."

Maura laughed. "They know, all right. They are simply biding their time."

"What do they look like?" KiKu asked.

Yeti shrugged her shoulders. "I do not know. I have never seen one."

"Are you sure Dorak is nowhere near us?" asked KiKu, disliking having no contact with his spy network.

"We have patrols throughout this area. It would be unlikely that Dorak could get by without our seeing him," answered Benzar.

KiKu gave him a disdainful look. "If it were only Dorak, I would rest easy, but the Black Cacodemon is another matter."

"You fear him?" Benzar asked.

"Yes, I fear him and so should you, my feathery friend, if you wish to stay alive."

"We had no knowledge of this sorcerer before the invasion," Yeti said, thinking this was a fine opportunity to get KiKu to talk freely. "Had you dealings with him before?"

"I saw him several times as a youth when he served as the main advisor to Zoar's father, Tnpothar. Then Tnpothar died, and Zoar made use of him for several years. That was when the Bhuttanians started on their quest for more territory. After that, the priest seemed to have vanished. I had forgotten about him."

"Zoar always headed west?" Yeti asked.

"Yes. My country was the first to fall under Bhuttanian aggression after Tnpothar unified all the steppe tribes. Hittal fell completely under their domination, and then Tnpothar stopped. He thought enough territory had been subjugated. He wanted to spend the remaining years of his life training promising candidates as bureaucrats to govern the new territory."

"But he was not successful, was he?" Benzar inquired.

KiKu shook his head. "The Bhuttanians are not suited to the intricacies of statecraft. Their culture is based solely on warfare. They can conquer, but once they take the land and its people, they don't know how to assimilate them other than by terrorizing them into submission."

Sighing, KiKu said, "That is what happened to my people. We were hard to vanquish and Zoar, after his father's death, just ground us into the dust until we no longer resisted. Of course, by that time there were very few of us left. Still, the Bhuttanians are more sophisticated than they once were."

Maura tried not to grimace, thinking of the dirty stink hole her palace had become with the Bhuttanians staying there.

Seeing Maura stifle a bitter smile, KiKu added quickly, "It is true, Great Mother. The Bhuttanians have come a long way. Look at how Dorak managed Hasan Daeg once he invaded. It was much less bloody than the old days, I assure you."

Maura turned her head away at the mention of Dorak's name. She did not want them to see her distress.

"Then what happened?" asked Yeti, not wishing KiKu to be diverted from his tale.

KiKu resumed his saga. "Zoar continued the policy of expansion."

"Never south or north or east, for that matter," Yeti stated as a matter of fact.

"It was always to the west."

"Do you know why?" Maura asked.

KiKu shrugged his shoulders. "It was the omens."

He looked at the group's confused faces. "The priests of Bhuttu always deemed the west as fortuitous."

"And the Black Cacodemon is the High Priest of Bhuttu," spat Maura, her hands balling into fists.

"Until he was banished from court by Zoar," concurred KiKu. "As I said before, this was the first time I had seen him since I was a child. I was surprised that Dorak summoned him. He must have been quite desperate."

Yeti thrust back her shoulders with fierce pride. "We are a hard race to defeat."

KiKu looked up at Yeti. "Madam, with that, I will give you no quarrel."

"Enough of this talk. Wake me up when the Lahorians decide to meet with us. As for me, I am going to take a nap," said Maura, strolling over to a tree that provided shade. She curled up in her armor on the ground and was soon asleep.

The hetmaan hid in a bush close enough to keep an eye on things while remaining out of sight.

Benzar and Yeti assumed places high in surrounding trees.

Yeti was disappointed that the conversation with KiKu was halted so abruptly. She felt Maura had done so on purpose. *Life is circles within circles*, thought Yeti as she watched over the Hasan Daegian queen and the enigmatic spylord.

9

Dorak angrily entered his tent.

The trail to the City of the Peaks had proved false, and he had wasted precious time searching for Maura. He threw off his gloves and kicked over a small table. Hearing a titter, Dorak looked toward the back of the tent.

The Black Cacodemon was just visible in the shadows, lurking there with his hands folded in the sleeves of his black velvet robe.

"What do you want?" barked Dorak, irritated at discovering the wizard in his private tent. "Have you found my wife?"

The Black Cacodemon solemnly nodded.

Dorak's heart beat faster at the answer. "Where? Tell me, you spawn of a demon! Where is she?"

"Do you wish to find her because of what she can

give us or because you still fancy her?" the sorcerer rasped.

"My motives do not concern you," replied Dorak hotly.

"I think they do, young master. For the use of my powers in conquering Hasan Daeg, you are in debt to me. It would not do to have you take pity on this wretch of a queen simply to placate your sense of morality."

Dorak growled, "I owe nothing! You are but a lowly servant to Bhuttu. It is through Bhuttu that you are granted powers, and Bhuttu has blessed me, not you."

The wizard bent over as though he suffered from pain. His black robe quivered until he threw back his head, snorting short bursts of sound.

Dorak realized the wizard was laughing.

"Oh, that is precious," giggled the sorcerer. "You actually think there is a Bhuttu, a god, who if placated, will grant your wishes. Dorak, I thought you were of different stuff, but you truly are just a superstitious peasant like your mother. You should have learned more from your father. He never believed in Bhuttu or in any god for that matter. Zoar thought it was all rot, stuff for the masses to swallow. He would have none of it. That's why he sent me away. He couldn't stomach the sight of me and refused to use my powers. He had his own power—the power of a strong will such as the world will never see again. He didn't need me ever."

The Black Cacodemon circled Dorak. "But you are made of weaker stuff. The Dinii and the Hasan Daegians routed your army like children breaking sticks. You couldn't think of how to destroy the wall of mist without magic. I could think of several ways to break down that sleepy border, but you panicked."

Dorak turned away from the magician.

The Black Cacodemon chuckled. "Yes, you panicked and summoned me to help you. Now you are in my debt and pay me, you shall."

"Or what?" asked Dorak hotly, lightly touching his sword's hilt.

"I will expose you as the murderer of your father."

"You can never prove that," Dorak contested fiercely.

The wizard waved his hand.

Before Dorak appeared the image of him murdering Zoar. His father struggled as Dorak, looking grim but determined, slowly suffocated him. Dorak turned away from the awful sight. "Stop tormenting me, you fiend!" he whimpered.

The wizard waved his hand again, and the image disappeared. "I may have done many evil things in my life, but I have never committed the crimes of patricide and regicide. Your soul must be very dark, and knowing

how your father loved you, the guilt must be unbeara-
ble."

Dorak grabbed the wizard by the throat.

The Black Cacodemon touched his amulet and vanished, leaving Dorak holding only air.

Hearing a gootee-like snort, Dorak swirled around.

The wizard was calmly sitting in a chair with his legs
crossed under his black robe. "You cannot kill me,"
declared the Black Cacodemon. "You are, how should I
put this, trapped, my dear boy." He uncrossed his legs
and leaned forward. "Because I am so fond of you,
Dorak, I am willing to make a deal that will outshine
your love for this girl."

"I'm listening."

"I have lived for a long, long time, but I wish to be
young in the flesh once again. The Bogazkoy can offer
that. I do not want to remain in this decrepit body for
my remaining years, which even without the Bogazkoy
are many. You are haunted by your crime to the point
that it is driving you slowly insane. I can help you with
that."

"How?" asked Dorak, suddenly interested.

"Get me to the Bogazkoy and help me persuade the
plant to accept me as the bonding mate rather than the
girl, and I will give you not only her, but I will erase any
memory of your crime. It will be as though you never

committed it. You will believe that Zoar died of natural causes like everyone else. You will live the rest of your life with the woman you treasure, sitting on the throne of the aga. You will be happy, secure, and without any painful memories to rob you of sleep in the middle of the night. Just think of it, Dorak. I'm offering you a freedom that all men dream about—freedom from one's past mistakes!"

Dorak stood, thinking the offer over carefully. It was very tempting, but could he trust this magician?

The wizard leaned closer and fingered the leather of Dorak's leggings. "Who knows, Dorak, when I am young again, we may find common attraction."

Dorak moved away from the wizened old man. "I choose my own bedmates, and you shall never be among them."

The Black Cacodemon shrugged his shoulders. "One can never know. Circumstances make strange bedfellows. Your job now is to find the Bogazkoy before the girl does."

"I thought you didn't know where she is."

"I do. She is at the Sacred Lake of Yappor. Look on your map. It is an insignificant lake in the middle of nowhere."

"The Hasan Daegians think it is inhabited by their nature goddess Mekonia. I wonder what Maura is doing there?" said Dorak, pouring over his maps.

"I do not think the Bogazkoy is there, but it is apparent she is waiting for something or someone."

"It will take days to get there from here."

"Get something to eat, rest while there is time, and gather your best men. I will prepare a spell to transport you. I must find out why your wife has gone there."

Dorak strode outside his tent and told Alexanee to gather twenty good men with horses and to wait by his tent in two hours time.

Alexanee pressed his fist to his chest and hurried to carry out Dorak's orders.

Hailing a slave, Dorak ordered food and drink brought to his tent. When Dorak reentered his tent, the Black Cacodemon was gone. It did not surprise him.

Just as well, thought Dorak, while pushing on the backside of a servant pulling his boots off.

10

Yeti shook Maura vigorously.

Maura struggled to open her eyes and leaned her head on her elbow.

"Get up! They come," said Yeti, pointing to the lake.

Maura sat up and shook the cobwebs from her head. "I don't know why I feel so sleepy," stated Maura as she struggled to get up. Her muscles were stiff and sore after sleeping in her armor.

"Did you drink from the lake?" asked Yeti, helping Maura to her feet.

"No, just from your waterskin."

Yeti glanced suspiciously at the sleeping Benzar snoring loudly and dangling upside down from a high branch. "I told that idiot to get water from the stream, not the lake."

"But it looks so clean and pure."

"And it puts you to sleep like the caromate plant does a foreigner."

"I've never slept so well in my life."

Yeti pointed to the lake. "Enough of this. Behold! The Lahorians come!"

KiKu joined Maura and Yeti on the sandy shore of the lake.

Despite the darkness that had fallen several hours ago, KiKu could see the water rolling and turning as though boiling in a kettle. Light streamed upward from the bottom of the lake. He had seen many wondrous things in his life, but he hoped his courage would not fail now as he watched hundreds of strobing, colored bubbles pop up from the surface and gently roll toward them.

Maura was both excited and fearful as she watched large spheres emerge from the turbulent water. She stole a glance at Yeti.

The proud hawk's human face was contorted by fear as she beheld her race's ancient enemy.

Maura realized that it required every ounce of Yeti's training to remain composed and firm in her stance.

Yeti stepped in front of Maura protectively as did Benzar, who had awakened and flown beside them.

Knowing this was not the time to confront the Dinii's protective attitude, Maura satisfied herself with a view stolen between the hawks as they stood akimbo in front of her.

She heard KiKu move to protect her flank. Giving him a quick look, she saw he had his sword out and was studying the forest behind them. Not wishing to have anyone with a sword near her back, she pulled out her dagger just in case.

As if hearing her thoughts, KiKu sheathed his sword but still watched the dark outline of the tall forest.

Yeti let out a sharp trill, and within seconds, fifty Dinii flew out of the forest and stood in a defensive ring around the Hasan Daegian queen and KiKu.

Maura smiled. She should have known Yeti would have more Dinii around in case there was trouble. Many of the Dinii she recognized from her days of living amongst them.

They did not turn in her direction but kept watch on the approaching bubbles. Each Dini had his or her deadly razor-sharp talons exposed.

Maura wondered if they blamed her for the destruction of their home or if they held Dorak responsible. She pushed the thought from her mind and concentrated on the bobbing orbs and the deafening thunder overhead. Rain began to pelt them in earnest.

The largest of the orbs rolled to the shore. It slowly dissipated, exposing a woman in its center. The woman stood naked with long brown hair covering her breasts. Neither her hair nor skin was wet from the tumultuous water crashing about her mid-thigh. The Lahorian woman looked like a Kaserian, except parts of her flesh were translucent, exposing her veins, ligaments, and muscles.

"Empress Maura, why do you hide behind the Dinii? Why do you insult us with your fear?" the woman shouted over the thunder.

Feeling ashamed, Maura pushed Yeti and Benzar aside and stepped in front of them.

The Lahorian woman bowed her head. "Greetings, Great Mother," she said, beckoning. "We are happy to meet with you at last, but we must hurry. The black-robed one knows of your presence and will soon approach now that we have arrived. Come with me so I may transport you below."

"What assurances do I have that you are a friendly force?" Maura shouted back over the howling wind.

"We are one." The woman held up her hands, revealing a single, blinking eye in each palm. "We have from the beginning orchestrated your upbringing." Her hair blew upward with the howling wind, exposing pendulous breasts.

Several spheres landed beside her and fell away, leaving two men standing on the water. They too held up their hands, exposing eyes in their palms.

Maura saw that their penises and testicles were small.

"You and your friend must come with us quickly. The Dinii are to join Iegani in the Forbidden Zone."

Yeti cried out, "We will not leave her unescorted. We must come with her!"

The woman shook her head. "We cannot accommodate any more than three. There is simply not enough oxygen. You may come, but you must order the rest of the Dinii to fly to the Forbidden Zone."

"My orders were that you were to smuggle her into Siva and then to the Forbidden Zone," yelled Yeti, testing her.

"That was the man named KiKu's plan. We will take her directly to the Forbidden Zone. The magician now knows where she is and is approaching fast. We must hurry." The woman beckoned to Maura again. "Join me!"

Maura looked into the stormy sky and at the chaotic water that was cresting high. She was fearful that she would drown but stepped toward the woman as water lapped at her leather boots. "You are taking me to Iegani?"

"We are taking you as far as we can in the Forbidden Zone. There, at a rendezvous spot, Iegani will have Dinii fly you into Atetelco."

"What is Atetelco?" Maura asked, pushing back the hair whipping in her face.

"It is the ancient capital of the Dinii. Iegani waits for you as does the Mother Bogazkoy."

Maura was not convinced.

The Lahorian woman looked into the sky, sensing the coming of Dorak and his minions on the wings of a spell. Time was running out. "Call for Iegani and see for yourself," the Lahorian cried out as a forceful wave crashed around her.

Maura, sensing the urgency of her decision, drew upon her inner strength. *Please don't fail me, Iegani,* she pleaded.

Go with her. Do all that she instructs. Hurry! The Black Cacodemon is coming with Dorak!

Maura heard Iegani's voice as though he were standing next to her. Her head snapped back, and her eyes rolled over in their sockets. She felt strong hands catch her.

Yeti knew Iegani's message had been powerful. She had no doubt it was Iegani who had touched the mind of Maura with such force. She had seen Maura in such trances before. Yeti lifted the girl in her arms and stepped up to the Lahorian woman, placing Maura at the woman's feet.

Without waiting for an invitation, KiKu jumped

next to one of the men who held a hand out to the hetmaan. An orb enveloped them while riding out into the lake.

Yeti hated water, but still strode out to the last remaining man. She stood knee deep in water when she felt something slide under her feet and raise her up. Sides of an iridescent bubble encircled her. She shouted to the rest of the Dinii, "We will meet in the Forbidden Zone!"

The words were no sooner uttered than the Dinii spread their wings and flew west.

Satisfied that her subordinates were safely on their way, Yeti began to investigate the bubble. She crunched her wings behind her and bent over as its structure was confining. "May I touch it?" she asked the amused Lahorian male who watched her expressions with curiosity.

"Gently," he clicked in the Dinii language.

Yeti made sure her talons were safely retracted before she gingerly placed the palm of her hand on the orb's transparent surface. It gave with a push. Slowly it began moving toward the center of the lake. Yeti saw the lit globe with the Lahorian woman and Maura descend into the water.

KiKu was also watching from his iridescent sphere and looked to Yeti for reassurance.

She smiled bravely and waved.

The sphere began bobbing over the steep waves. The jostling threw Yeti against the side while the Lahorian man remained stable. Sensing Yeti's discomfort with water, he sought to comfort her by speaking, "Perhaps it will help if you sit down."

Yeti agreed and slid down the flexible, iridescent sides of their globe. She heard a grinding sound and noticed the orb moved at right angles and wondered if something was pulling it. Exploring the transparent floor, Yeti thought she might discover a chain or rope but could see nothing.

"Where are we going?"

"We travel directly to the rendezvous spot to meet with the Divigi while bypassing our city."

"Why is that?" Yeti asked.

"Because we will be under attack in a few seconds, and we wish to draw conflict away from our homes." The Lahorian man pointed to the sky above them.

Yeti looked up through a circular window. The sky was no longer streaked with lightning as before, but now had a strange green and purple hue. She had seen the sky like that before. She threw herself against the sphere. "We must get out! The Black Cacodemon is here!"

The Lahorian male touched Yeti's arm, and she fell

silent. "There, there," cooed the Lahorian soothingly. "We will be safe."

"We will?" Yeti asked incredulously, feeling ashamed at her outburst.

The Lahorian male nodded and said, "We are one, and we are powerful together. He will not breach us. I must join the others now. We must concentrate." He closed his eyes and held up his closed palms, which slowly opened to expose its eyes.

The frightened Dini watched KiKu's sphere disappear into the murky depths. Her sphere kept moving on the surface until it reached the spot where the other bubbles had disappeared. With a low humming sound, it slowly began to descend.

Yeti could see glowing balls of a purplish green light explode in the water, lashing against the sides of the orb. Yeti peered toward the shore. She made out the figures of Dorak astride a prancing warhorse, and the Black Cacodemon standing in the water hurling angry-looking balls of energy.

As water rushed to cover the top of her descending bubble, Yeti smiled and whispered, "You lost again, Dorak."

11

Maura came to her senses.

Halfway down to the bottom of the lake, she sat up with a start and looked around. The first thing she saw was the legs of her benefactor. The Lahorian's legs were hairless, and her paper-thin skin was covered with shimmering oil. Maura could plainly make out the woman's muscles and veins.

Maura shuddered and drew herself into a ball so she would not make contact with the Lahorian who was deep in a self-induced trance. Wiping condensation off the inside wall, she peered outside.

Hundreds of spheres were moving in the water. They were different colors and sizes—each creating its own illumination and transporting Lahorians. Smaller bubbles of pale blues and green hovered about the spheres, providing light in the now dark murky water.

Maura moved around the Lahorian woman. She could plainly see the two orbs carrying KiKu and Yeti, both of whom had hunkered down trying to find room in a bubble that was too small. They both looked miserable but determined.

Yeti glanced in her direction, and Maura waved to her. Yeti waved back and cupped her hands over her mouth yelling something.

Maura put a hand to her ear, trying to indicate that she could not hear.

Yeti began pointing frantically to the bottom of the orb.

Maura looked down.

To the right, at the bottom of the lake, was a collection of illuminated spheres stacked on top of each other. Covering the entire structure was a giant bubble with multi-colored veins that blinked off and on. The conglomeration of stacked bubbles resembled fish eggs.

Maura could see outlines of people moving around inside in various compartments. As she wondered if her group was going to the strange Lahorian city, her bubble veered off to the left. The other orbs floating beside moved also. They picked up speed and descended ever deeper into the lake. Maura could see large schools of fish dart about trying to get out of the spheres' way.

Occasionally, a monstrous fish with large sharp teeth would deliberately swim to the bubble, trying to bite into the sphere's fabric. Disgruntled, the large predators swam off only to attack a smaller bubble, which acted as a decoy.

Yeti did not like these fish and bared her teeth at them, making a great commotion in her bubble.

Still, the Lahorians did not awaken from their self-induced trances.

Resigned to her fate, Maura lay down on the floor and contented herself with wondering at the various life forms that swam past the speeding orbs.

Without warning, bolts of purple energy sliced through the deep water. Some of the bolts hit the orbs with great force, causing them to vibrate violently.

Maura feared they would start leaking, but they did not. She looked back and saw many of the spheres hit by angry lightning, but these attacks did not disturb the spheres' progress. Maura discerned the distant city was under attack also. A blanket of green light enveloped the city and furiously lashed out in the shape of a fist at the stacked spheres, trying to find a weak point.

Whoever the Lahorians were, they were risking their lives to save her skin. Maura was grateful and wished she could help her companion, but she knew that her ministrations would be weak help indeed.

She would just have to wait.

12

Dorak jumped off his black steed.

He hurled himself at the Black Cacodemon, hitting the old man with such a blow that they both fell to the ground.

The sorcerer opened his eyes under the hood of his cowl, exhaling loudly. Angrily, he sat up and raised a finger that released a short blast of energy at Dorak.

Dorak could not rise.

The lances of Dorak's soldiers pointed immediately at the wizard's heart. The Black Cacodemon smiled and lowered his hand, sitting very still.

An officer helped a stunned Dorak to his feet.

"Dorak, we almost had her," the wizard whined.

Dorak shook the dirt off his pants and tunic, not bothering to hide his disgust. "We were only to find Empress Maura."

"It was my plan to capture her and make her lead us to the Bogazkoy."

"By drowning her?"

"I don't need that bothersome girl anyway to accomplish my task. I know how to manipulate the Tree of Life."

"But I want her, you idiot! Alive and well. Not lying dead on the bottom of some lake."

"Details," chirped the wizard, fluttering his hand like an injured bird.

Dorak paced back and forth studying the lake while the violent rain stopped.

His soldiers scouted the shores and reported back to him. Others made makeshift rafts and, guided by the light of oil torches, paddled their way across the lake and back.

Dorak leaned against his horse. "Tell me, Magician, did you think you were going to find the empress in a soap bubble with naked people?"

The soldiers had allowed the Black Cacodemon to sit on a leather-folding stool but watched him warily. He turned his head from the lake toward Dorak. Dawn was coming, and the sun was emerging from behind the forest trees, casting a soft yellow glow.

"I must admit that I am confounded," confessed the Black Cacodemon.

Dorak seemed surprised at the wizard's candor and was about to speak when several of his scouts appeared.

The scouts fell to their knees. "Great Aga, we have navigated the lake."

"What did you find?"

"Nothing. No horse tracks but ours, though we did see footprints of the Dinii."

"It was expected they might be here. What else?"

"The lake is not a closed system. There is an underground river which flows to the northwest."

"The west," murmured Dorak. "Always the west. Does the river ever surface?"

"Yes, Great Aga. If our maps are correct, the river should surface in about a hundred miles."

"That is where we shall probably pick up their trail," Dorak reasoned excitedly. "Don't you agree?" He turned toward the Black Cacodemon, but the magician was no longer sitting placidly on his stool. He was nowhere to be seen.

Dorak roared, "Blast it! He's gone on ahead—that snake charmer." Jumping on his horse, he spurred it, causing the horse to spin into a gallop.

The tired and famished scouts had no choice but to follow.

13

Maura must have fallen asleep.

When she awoke, she was still in the orb, and the Lahorian woman was kneeling over her.

"You are pregnant," the Lahorian stated flatly.

Maura nodded. "It is the aga's child."

"That is good. We were worried you might conceive by the Dinii prince."

Blushing deeply, Maura tried to hide her embarrassment by looking out of the sphere.

"We are in the river system now," said the Lahorian.

Maura turned her head and gaped. Realizing the Lahorian woman studied her as well, Maura stammered, "I . . . I am very sorry. I didn't mean to stare."

The Lahorian sat down beside the young woman, leaning against the back of the humming sphere. "It is all right. We know we appear strange to you. My name used to be Rakel. Now we are simply known as the Lahorians to you."

Maura was pensive for a moment but brightened. "You no longer have an individual identity?"

"Correct, Great Mother of Hasan Daeg. We used to be separate, but now we are one."

"Why are you helping me?"

"We are reaching the end of our journey to a spiritual union. We do not wish this process to be interfered with by outsiders. It's in our best interest to help those who would wish us well on our journey."

"How does that involve me?"

"With you as ruling empress, there would be policies that could protect our homeland. You have not seen the destruction in the mountains. The Bhuttanians have great need of timber and have been stripping entire mountains of trees. The dirt from the slopes contaminates the streams, which feed this lake. See for yourself. The river used to be clear. For now, we have enough muscular strength to build the machines needed to cleanse the river before it spills into our lake, but it will not always be so. Even now our arms atrophy."

It was true. Maura noted that the Lahorian's arms looked weak compared to her muscular ones.

"The Bhuttanians must assimilate into the Hasan Daegian culture, or they must be destroyed," Rakel said emphatically. "You must join with the Mother Bogaz-koy. Only then will you have the power to fight the one known as the Black Cacodemon."

"My mother fused with an offspring of the Bogaz-koy, and she did not have the strength to fight Dorak and his pet sorcerer."

"The Royal Bogazkoy was ill and dying. The Mother Bogazkoy is a thousand times more potent than her offspring. Only you possess what the Mother Bogazkoy needs. Neither the Black Cacodemon nor Dorak will suit the needs of the Mother."

Maura struggled to talk about the Bogazkoy. She remembered being enveloped by the plant's tentacles, which had probed her every orifice. She sighed with pleasure at the thought of the plant's leaves caressing her skin and feeling tiny pinpricks as the leaves moved over her skin only to inject a blue substance into her skin. It had given her a feeling of euphoria she had never known.

"I don't understand. Why my family? Why not any female?"

The Lahorian smiled softly. "It is my guess that the Mother selected your ancestor out of personal prefer-ence. The Mother was attracted."

Maura was confused. "How can a plant have prefer-ences?"

"This is not just any plant. It is a Bogazkoy."

Still not understanding, Maura's mind raced, trying to connect all the Lahorian was telling her and what her mother had said.

The Lahorian looked at her as though watching her child take a first step.

Maura felt entirely stupid. She was not connecting the information. Maura was shocked by her lack of knowledge.

"You see, the title Mother Bogazkoy is a misnomer. It is both a she and a he." The Lahorian stopped to let this information sink in. "And it needs a Hasan Daegian queen's egg to reproduce."

Maura's eyes lightened with understanding. "My egg?"

The Lahorian placed her hand tenderly on Maura's shoulder. "My dear, it will need most of your eggs."

14

Maura's brow furrowed.

"My eggs! You surely jest."

The Lahorian woman's eyes saddened. "You are young, and this news is a shock. I am sorry, but this is the way of the Mother Bogazkoy. We all have to sacrifice. That's why Hasan Daegian queens have only one child. The Bogazkoy only leaves the donor two eggs."

"You mean the Royal Bogazkoy was half Hasan Daegian?"

"The plant takes plasma from the queen's unfertilized eggs. The Bogazkoy is nothing more than a highly-evolved, sentient plant."

Maura instinctively put her hands on her belly. "What about my baby?"

Rakel spoke her words tenderly. "I do not know.

Tell the Mother you are pregnant and ask it to be merciful. It was always our plan that your baby should live and rule both Hasan Daeg and Bhuttan, but with the Mother Bogazkoy, who knows."

"I won't go. I won't do anything to hurt my baby!" Maura barked stubbornly.

"If this is your wish, no one can force you. You must go willingly to the Bogazkoy or else it will not accept you. However, if you don't, then the Black Cacodemon will surely intercede with magic and deceive the Bogazkoy to gain the plant's injection of its sap. No one will be able to stop the Black Cacodemon then. He will be too powerful. This unholy union will plague our descendants for generations to come until our people die out. The planet will be uninhabitable, and no one will survive but those the Black Cacodemon wills. Is this what you want for our future? For your child's future?"

Maura slid down the wall of the pulsating sphere and cried softly. She threw off the comforting hand of Rakel.

The Lahorian did not touch her again, leaving the young woman alone with her private thoughts.

Terrible images ran through Maura's mind as she tried to sort through her options. All she knew was that she wanted to run away and hide from Dorak and the Lahorians. Both of their needs were too great for her to bear. She did not speak to Rakel. Around and around Rakel's words spun in her head. *We all have to sacrifice!* Maura could stand the silence no longer. "What have you sacrificed, Rakel?" she asked sarcastically.

The Lahorian wiped condensation off the side of the sphere and touched Maura's forehead with the cool wetness. "This sphere was damaged during the attack by the Black Cacodemon and is no longer watertight. There is just enough oxygen to get you to the rendez-vous spot, but I will not be able to return home."

Maura was alarmed. "The Dinii will fly you to safe-ty."

The Lahorian shook her head slowly. "I'm afraid not. My people have not left the water for over three hundred years. Our bones are brittle. No matter how careful the Dinii are, this frail body would never survive the journey home. Without the sphere, we cannot survive outside of our city."

She folded her hands together. "It does not matter. We have foreseen this death before you were born. We even discussed it with Gitar."

"You visited Gitar?"

"She came to us years ago. We showed your adoptive mother the future. She knew the death of her world was imminent. She was frightened as you are now, but she was determined that you should survive to carry out your destiny. Now you must take up where she left off. Let us show you how it could be." Rakel extended her arms and held her palms up. The eyes in the middle of her palms opened their lids sleepily and blinked several times. "Look into the future and see your destiny."

Standing transfixed, Maura stared into the seeing eyes of Rakel. Deeper and deeper she felt pulled until she was no longer in the sphere but sitting on a horned throne in the middle of a massive pavilion. Torches held in brass sconces lit the dank leather shelter giving it a shadowy and smoky atmosphere.

Standing by Maura's side was an older Yeti whose feathers were tinged with grey. A young girl whose skin was pale blue and whose hair was ebony stood on the other. She had Dorak's black, probing eyes. The young girl slowly turned her head and looked at Maura.

She saw herself smile at the girl and then turn her attention to the multitude prostrating themselves before them: Bhuttanians, Hasan Daegians, Sivans, Kittium, Hittals, and other races that Maura did not recognize.

That is my daughter, Maura heard herself say somewhere in the distance.

That is the daughter that could be, if only you would speak to the Mother Bogazkoy, she heard Rakel speak into in her mind.

The image blurred and wavered as though it was a

mirage in the desert. Then it disappeared.

Maura stood unsteadily in the cramped sphere. She placed her hands on her belly and locked eyes with Rakel. "Do not be afraid, Rakel. I will have this baby, and then I will restore order to Kaseri."

"You know what you have to do to gain the throne?"

"I understand my destiny. I know what it is that you would have of me."

"It will be a sorrowful occasion."

"What do any of you care except that I do as you wish? Was that not the reason for my birth? To do everyone's dirty work for them?"

"I am truly sorry, but what you say has merit. No one else could have gotten close enough to the aga, whether he be Zoar or Dorak."

"But then the Black Cacodemon intervened."

"He was unforeseen by us. He managed to keep his presence a secret from us."

"Clever," mused Maura. "But I was to marry Dorak and conceive his child."

Rakel beamed a strange smile. "Well, conceive Zoar's or Dorak's child anyway."

Maura's eyes darkened. "It didn't matter if I were forced."

Rakel's face paled as she looked away. "It did not

matter to us how the child was conceived."

"The only thing that mattered was that an aga and I meet, conceive, and bear the child who would one day rule over Hasan Daeg and Bhuttan, thus ensuring friendly policies to the Lahorians. And if I had to kill the child's father, so be it," Maura spat into the sphere. "You Lahorians are really smarmy."

Rakel ignored the insults in Maura's words. "It is more complicated than you imagine. We are but a spoke in the wheel."

Maura growled, "But something went wrong with your plans. The great all-seeing eyes failed in projecting the future because the Black Cacodemon eluded you. You didn't foresee that I would fall in love with Dorak and would shudder at the thought of harming him."

"We did not foresee that he would fall in love with you."

"You mean he loves me?" Maura clasped her hands together.

"That does not change what you must do."

"If I could talk to Dorak without the Black Caco-demon, I could make him see. We could do away with that wicked man."

Shaking her head slowly, Rakel began to tremble. "It is not possible. You are thinking like an impetuous girl, not a queen."

"You mean I am thinking with hope?"

"The hope in your love is not possible. You are thinking without clarity. Once Dorak takes you back to Bhuttan, it would only be a matter of time before you and the child are assassinated. The Bhuttanians want a Bhuttanian for their queen."

"But Dorak has never married a Bhuttanian. He first married that Anqarian woman."

"And as you saw with your own eyes, he did not acknowledge her or his first son."

"That was because of me."

"NO! You must listen to us. He has never acknowledged her publicly nor his son for he does not want this child to rule."

Maura put her hands over her ears. "Lies! Lies! He loves me. He will not hurt me. You said so yourself."

"We said he loves you. We did not say he would not harm you. He has never been honest with you."

"It's not true. Not true."

"You know it is true. No matter how much Dorak loves you, he is ambitious and desires to rule above all else. He will not let his love for you interfere with his ultimate goal."

Maura faced the Lahorian. "Tell me one thing. Did Dorak know that Mikkotto had set a trap for my mother?"

"We cannot lie. Dorak had no knowledge of Mik-kotto's treachery."

Sighing with relief, Maura mumbled, "Thank you for that."

The orb lurched forward, throwing both Maura and Rakel off balance and causing them to fall against the side of the sphere. It twisted and spun, finally ramming itself into the soft mud of the riverbank.

Maura fell on Rakel and immediately pulled herself up. She instinctively felt her stomach and, sensing that everything was fine, turned her attention to Rakel.

Rakel's face twisted in agony.

Maura realized that Rakel had taken a nasty fall.

Murky water seeped into the sphere.

Kneeling down, Maura felt for any broken bones or injuries to Rakel.

The Lahorian woman groaned with each touch.

"I'm sorry," Maura said as she continued to explore the woman's body.

"I have not been touched since I suckled my child," moaned Rakel.

"How long ago was that?" asked Maura, trying to keep Rakel talking.

"Sixteen years."

"Why does that not surprise me," retorted Maura, checking the woman's arms.

"We are not affectionate with the flesh. Just the mind."

The water in the sphere was rising higher until the tops of Maura's boots were covered. "Let me heal you," Maura offered.

"Too much damage. Will weaken you. You must get to the Forbidden Zone."

Maura held the woman's head out of the water. She could see that Rakel was hemorrhaging from the lungs. Blood seeped under the skin of her chest and spread into her abdomen.

Rakel coughed, and a thin trickle of blood appeared at the corner of her colorless lips. "Save yourself," she implored.

Righting herself, Maura felt the sides of the sphere. Sunlight poured through the crystalline bubble. Maura recognized part of the sphere was out of the water. If they could break out, land would only be a step away. Maura pounded on the top of the bubble. "How do we get out of this thing?"

Choking on water rising over her mouth, Rakel struggled to point her finger at something but dropped it from exhaustion.

Maura hunkered down again and pulled Rakel up into a sitting position.

Rakel cried out from the pain. Her entire chest was

red, and the crimson stain was gathering in her belly.

Maura knew Rakel's end was coming.

Rakel struggled for air. "The walls are giving way and will collapse. As I die, so does the sphere."

"You mean this thing is alive?"

The injured woman nodded weakly. "Do not fear. The others are on their way."

"Do you realize that you have been saying 'I' instead of 'we'?"

Smiling faintly, Rakel coughed, spewing out a spray of blood.

Maura tried to wipe the blood from the woman's face, but Rakel weakly pushed her hand away. Her lips began to pull back from her teeth, and her eyes were becoming dimmer. "It is a bit of vanity that I allow with my passing." She locked eyes with Maura. "May Mekonia be with you on your difficult journey. I can be of no more help."

Maura started to reply when Rakel shook with the death rattle and lay still. She gently closed the Lahorian's eyes and wiped the blood from around her mouth. Grateful that Rakel did not suffer long, Maura turned her attention to the orb. Taking a dagger out of her boot, Maura stabbed the sphere repeatedly.

Water began to pour in rapidly, and Maura now stood waist deep in it. The sphere shook and shuddered as Maura tried to twist its skin off. The bubble began to lose its iridescent illumination, but its sides still would not yield.

Maura breathed deep gulps of air even though she knew she was using up her oxygen supply.

A large object bumped into the sphere, knocking Maura over into the pooling water. Hearing shouts, Maura yelled in response as she tried not to step on Rakel's body.

Dark forms climbed over the top of the orb and tore at it. Finally, a razor-sharp talon ripped the top of the sphere, and Yeti's head appeared through the opening.

Seeing Maura was safe, her face lit up until she spied the dead body of Rakel. "My oarsman told me she had died, and you were unable to open this contraption because it had died with her."

"Oarsman?" echoed Maura.

"That's what I call the Lahorian. Come on. I'll help you out," Yeti said, extending her hand through the torn skin of the sphere.

Maura tried to pull Rakel out of the water. "Help me with her!"

Yeti waved her hand. "Leave her be. Each Lahorian has an orb in which they are buried. The Lahorians will take it back with them. Come on. She's beyond our help now."

Maura hesitated.

"She knew she was going to die on this trip. She foretold it many years ago to your mother just as she foretold your mother's death."

Maura reluctantly let Rakel's body slide back into the cold water.

She stood on her toes catching Yeti's hand and was pulled up. Once through the hole and outside, she sat on top of the bubble while her eyes adjusted to the bright light.

"It's early morning. We've traveled all night."

Maura cupped her hand over her eyes and scanned her surroundings. "Where's KiKu?"

"Here I am, Great Mother," greeted a relieved KiKu, standing on the riverbank.

"The woman is gone. She bled to death."

"Yes, we know. The other Lahorians felt her death. We were following at a distance and hurried as fast as we could."

"Where are the Lahorians?"

KiKu pointed toward the middle of the river. "They are mourning their companion."

Maura's gaze followed the direction of his finger to where two large glittering spheres bobbed in the river. She could barely make out the darkened forms of two men who seemed to be chanting.

"They will take her back when we leave," said Yeti, watching them also.

"Should we stay and help them?" asked Maura, uncomfortable with leaving Rakel's body submerged in the water.

"They are waiting for us to go. They do not wish us to observe their death ritual. Besides, we have a journey of our own." Yeti looked up into the sky. "We must be off if we are to meet Iegani at the rendezvous point."

Maura looked at Yeti, disbelieving. "This isn't it?"

Yeti answered calmly. "We are in the Forbidden Zone but several miles short of our destination. Your orb ran into a log and got snagged. The Lahorian was hurt so she couldn't maneuver it out." She shrugged her massive shoulders. "So here we are."

"Can you fly us there, Yeti?" asked KiKu.

"Not at the moment. My wings are cramped from being inside that tiny thing for so long. I would probably drop you."

Maura jumped off the top of the sphere and onto the shore. Her legs had muscle cramps, and her leather clothes were becoming extremely uncomfortable after being exposed to water. She took her dagger and split the sides of her pants and then stretched her leggings around her legs.

After KiKu handed her a waterskin, she took a long

drink. Sheathing her dagger, Maura massaged her calves and then straightened. "Let's be off," she ordered with determination, trying to ignore her growling stomach.

"This way," Yeti advised as she set off at a brisk pace.

Glancing back at the spheres in the water one more time, Maura set off after Yeti with KiKu following her. They stayed close to the riverbank, making sure they never lost sight of it. After several miles, they finally came to a small clearing.

Yeti stopped and surveyed the trees.

Maura and KiKu hid in the bushes until Yeti gave them the signal that it was safe.

Satisfied, Yeti stepped out into the clearing and began stretching her wings. "Ah, that feels good," she said to no one in particular.

"Where are the others?" asked KiKu, surveying his surroundings suspiciously.

"We are to be picked up here. We simply wait," replied Yeti, scanning the sky.

KiKu merely grunted and fished in his pockets for some biscuits, which he shared with Yeti and Maura. Stale though they were, Maura was grateful for anything to eat.

They had not been waiting long when Yeti heard the familiar flapping of great wings from the western sky. It was mid-afternoon. "Right on time," she said, checking the position of the sun in the sky.

Three hawks settled lightly on their feet.

Though KiKu should have been getting used to the sight of the Dinii, they nevertheless astonished him. He unwillingly took a step back.

All three Dinii bowed very low to Maura and greeted her with various hoots and whistles particular to the Dinii language.

Maura inclined her head toward the hawks while a frown spread across her face. "Greetings, Toppo," she said, thinking of their last encounter. "I hear you have the makings of a divigi."

Toppo blinked heavily. "You are most kind in your praise."

"Benzar. Tarsus."

"Always a pleasure, Great Mother."

Yeti interrupted. "We must be off. Benzar, you take KiKu. Tarsus, take Her Majesty."

Maura strode behind Tarsus.

He had a harness that she put around them both and buckled around his middle.

Maura placed her hands around Tarsus' neck and nestled between his wings as they took off with astounding speed.

Toppo took wing after them, protecting their flank.

KiKu searched the sky and saw more Dinii diving from cloud cover and quickly surrounding Tarsus and his passenger.

Grinning, Benzar went over to KiKu and turned his back, pointing to a harness.

KiKu paled, and his knees buckled. "I don't think I can do this again."

"You are the hetmaan who tricked Zoar. Surely, a ride on my back is nothing compared to dumping Zoar off his horse," needled Benzar.

"As long as I do not end up like Zoar."

"That's enough," commanded Yeti. She gathered some tall grass and quickly wove a strip that was long enough to go around KiKu's eyes and tied it behind his head. She did not even give KiKu a chance to protest. She covered his eyes and lifted the protesting KiKu into the harness. Seeing that he was becoming more and more agitated, she struck him sharply in the head, knocking him unconscious.

Benzar laughed.

Angry, Yeti swung Benzar around. "The last person who was afraid to ride a Dini had her neck broken. Don't you remember?"

Benzar's laughter suddenly stopped as he lowered his head. "I remember Mehmet," he said softly. "I meant no slight."

"Make sure this one arrives alive," snapped Yeti, her nerves frayed. The responsibility of Maura's safety was a heavy burden.

"Yes, Yeti," replied Benzar, his head cowed. He checked the harness and made sure KiKu was safely buckled in before spreading his wings and flying toward the western horizon.

As soon as Benzar was out of sight, fifty Dinii dove from under cloud cover and reported to Yeti. They brought water and food. Once Yeti satisfied her thirst and hunger, she rested in a large tree with the Dinii acting as guards. The first rest she had taken in many days was like a balm to her racing mind.

Night fell too quickly, and a guard awakened her. Groggily, she shook her head and splashed water on her face from a waterskin hanging on a branch. She shook her wings trying to work out the kinks and cramps until she was ready.

Standing in formation, the fifty-one Dinii took off in perfect unison and flew to join Iegani, the Great Divigi, waiting in Atetelco.

15

It grew bitterly cold.

Tarsus flew over the mountains that divided Hasan Daeg and the Forbidden Zone where Atetelco stood.

Huge goosebumps rose on Maura's skin as her teeth chattered. The wind howled in her face as she began to lose feeling in her extremities.

Hearing her moan, Tarsus thought he might lose her to the cold elements. He signaled to the other Dinii flying in formation with him, and they landed on a mountain. The Dinii carefully unbuckled the nearly unconscious Maura and laid her on the ground. Tarsus dug a hole in the snow while other Dinii rubbed Maura's skin vigorously. When they finished with the pit, several Dinii climbed in, and Tarsus lowered the shivering woman to them. They laid her on top of them as other Dinii climbed in and surrounded her, spreading their wings over her wet, cold body. Tarsus packed dry snow around them, leaving several air holes. Then he and the other Dinii buried themselves in the snow to wait for better weather.

Several Dinii hid among the mountain boulders to keep watch. They knew Iegani would be furious with this delay, but a late queen was better than a dead one.

As soon as dawn broke, Toppo lifted up from her shallow pit and faced the morning light. It was snowing heavily. She found that her water had frozen. Toppo broke the ice with her fist and she, along with several Dinii, breathed on the waterskin until the ice turned to slush.

Taking a pink powder from one of the many pouches hanging around her hips, she mixed the powder with the icy slush. The novice divigi located the spot where Maura was buried and dug until she unearthed the small group that was keeping the queen alive with their body heat.

The Dinii sleepily opened their eyes and yawned.

Toppo and Tarsus pulled them out of the pit along with the groggy but warm Maura.

Maura struggled to open her eyes as the Dinii gathered around to shield her from the extreme wind and the blanket of snow that was quickly covering them.

Toppo grabbed Maura's face with her powerful

hands and compelled her mouth to open. Pouring the pink ice water into Maura's mouth, Toppo stroked her throat forcing the liquid down.

Struggling for a moment, Maura swallowed and soon fell into a deep sleep. Checking the young woman's hands and feet, Toppo was satisfied there was no damage from frostbite and helped Tarsus harness Maura onto his back.

"Will she be all right?" Tarsus asked, more than a little concerned. He hated to face Iegani's wrath.

"She is warm. The powder will make her sleep the rest of the journey. She will not suffer from the cold anymore."

"Do you think KiKu is still alive?"

"I'm going back to find Benzar's party and see."

"Who would think these creatures would be so susceptible to a blizzard?"

Toppo wiped the snow from her eyelids. "We should have thought of it, even someone with Maura's strength."

All the other Dinii hopped around and shook the snow and ice from their wings, preparing to fly northwest. They stretched and rubbed their wings.

"As soon as they can accompany you, take off and don't stop until you reach the city," Toppo commanded. "We have only one more day."

Tarsus nodded, realizing the severity of the situation. He looked very concerned.

Toppo smiled, giving him a knowing look. "Don't worry. We will prevail." She patted his hand. Approaching an overhang, she spread her wings and took off into the howling wind.

Tarsus could not see her in the blinding snow but sensed her flying steadily into the wind. He turned and barked orders.

The other Dinii quickly gathered into formation. With the snow falling around them, they spread their mighty wings and flew into the western sky. Next stop would be the former capital of the Dinii. They were all determined to get there or die trying.

16

Maura awoke.

Her vision clouded as she struggled to focus on something white and fuzzy near her face. Finally, she relaxed and breathed a sigh of relief. "Hello, Iegani," she greeted huskily, her throat parched from her journey.

Iegani gently lifted her head and placed a bowl of warm water to her lips.

She drank greedily. When satisfied, she laid her head back on the pillow and closed her eyes.

"None of that," spat Iegani, shaking her shoulders. "Arise, young de Magela and face your destiny."

"What, no breakfast first?"

"Your Majesty, time is almost up. You must proceed to the Mother Bogazkoy now!"

Maura raised herself up on one elbow and squinted

at the blue-robed figure wringing her hands behind Iegani. "Ah, Noabini, the High Priestess of the House of Magi. How nice to see you. I wondered what had happened to you during all these months while your women suffered at the hands of the Bhuttanians." Maura leaned back down on the pillow and turned over, pulling the fur covers over her ears.

The High Priestess from the House of Magi and Iegani exchanged anxious glances.

Iegani tore off the cover and gave Maura a sharp kick in the leg. "Get up, you impertinent child. The future depends on our actions today."

Maura laughed, which soon turned into coughing. She spat a wad of pink phlegm, which landed precariously near Iegani's feet. She wiped her mouth with the back of her hand. "Don't you dare order me about, you old fraud. You lied to me about Dorak."

The priestess reacted harshly to Maura's words.

"Do I offend you, Priestess, when I tell you this nasty old birdman is a liar and a manipulator?" Maura spat.

Iegani gave her a withering glare.

Maura stretched out on the bed designed as a nest. "So this is the Forbidden City of the Overlords. I should say 'past' Overlords."

Iegani reached down and grabbed Maura by the hair.

"Stop!" Familiar hands pulled Maura away.

Maura blinked several times before she realized who held her. "Empress!" she whispered.

Empress Gitar kissed Maura's cheek and then held her tightly in her arms. "My lost chick. You've had to endure so much," she cooed. She cradled Maura in her strong arms and rocked her as though she were still a baby. "I'm sorry. Many have died and for what? A crazy man's ambition. It is so senseless." Setting Maura upright on her knees, Gitar extended her talons and began raking the tangles out of Maura's hair.

"The Lahorian, Rakel, is dead," mumbled Maura, leaning against Gitar. Maura enjoyed the touch of a familiar and kind hand.

Gitar stopped combing for a second and sighed deeply. "It is as she foretold."

Maura turned toward Gitar and grabbed her hand. "Did you know about the Mother Bogazkoy?"

Her large yellow eyes were full of pity as they locked with Maura's. "Not until years after we made the pact with the Lahorians. Rakel told me some of the mysteries of the Mother Bogazkoy, but not all."

"There is more?"

"Yes, more than you can dream of."

Iegani pointed a finger at Maura, whereas Gitar shot him a look of extreme displeasure. He ignored her stare and addressed Maura. "If you hate, then hate me. If you must have vengeance, kill me. I am the one who has brought much of this to pass, not Gitar."

Pushing Gitar's gentle hands away, Maura stood defiantly before Iegani. "Once my teacher. Now my enemy."

Iegani peered down at Maura. He tucked his wings submissively. "I am not your enemy, but I am not your friend. I have protected you, taught you, yes, even manipulated you. Not because I loved you, but because you were needed. Why, might you ask? I have no great faith in slave flesh."

Maura stiffened at the mention of the word "slave."

"Iegani," cautioned Gitar, "you go too far."

"You are the descendant of slaves we conquered and took to Hasan Daeg after the Lahorians defeated us. We needed beings to cultivate the land and tend to the forests so we could be free to pursue whatever we fancied. And if game was scarce, your kind nourished us." Iegani paused and took in the silence of the cavernous room. "As your kind developed, we granted you more privileges, but never doubt this," he waved a finger in Maura's face, "we were always in charge."

"You are hideous." Maura seethed with white-hot anger.

"No, I am practical."

"Why are you saying such things?" Gitar lamented. "Hasan Daegians have not been eaten for centuries ever since we made the treaty with them. Why do you try to inflame her?"

"Because I am sick of her sniveling and crawling before the Bhuttanians. Somewhere there is a queen inside her." He threw a goblet at Maura, spilling its contents and almost hitting Gitar in the shoulder. "A queen who will fight!" he roared. "Not this coward, this whining mass of putrid skin. She is playing games because she is mad at me. Well, you shame us. You shame your mother. You are nothing like her. You are a disgrace to Abisola's memory!"

Maura flailed her arms trying to get at Iegani, but Gitar held her fast. "I'm not a coward! I want to save my baby. And I'll tell you one thing, I never saw my mother out on the battlefield. It was me taking risks, putting my neck on the line!"

"Do you think the Black Cacodemon will let you have your baby if he finds you? You stupid child. He'll rip that baby from your womb and eat it with relish."

"And the Mother Bogazkoy might kill my baby as well."

Gitar tried to calm Maura down. "You don't know that."

"Can you guarantee that it won't?"

Gitar was quiet for a moment and then spoke carefully. "No, I can't. The only thing I know for sure is that the Black Cacodemon will soon be here, and if he reaches the Bogazkoy first, all is lost. For your baby, for my son, for everyone."

Gitar slowly knelt before the young queen. "I am begging for the lives of my people as well as your offspring. Take the one chance offered to you and mate with the Mother Bogazkoy. Please!"

Maura could not stand to see her mentor and sovereign on her knees. "Don't, please," she pleaded, helping Gitar to rise.

She turned to Iegani standing by watching, unmoved. "You think me a worthless queen, a young woman whose mind and heart have been muddled by selfishness and cowardice. My mind has been strained, but not by weakness. I thought I could reach Dorak."

Maura could see she was not influencing Iegani. "You don't understand. Haven't you ever been in love? Are you so old that you have forgotten its hold on the heart?"

Iegani was so taken aback by the questions that his feathers ruffled on his shoulders. He decided to ignore the subject. "You have been trained from birth to do your duty in anticipation of this very moment. The Lahorians foresaw you with a child. There is every reason to believe that the Mother Bogazkoy will not harm it. But we must go now!"

Maura felt Gitar standing protectively near her.

"Maybe there is another way?" said Gitar.

Iegani bellowed, "There is no other way! If there were, don't you think I would have thought of it?"

Resigned, Maura put her hand on Gitar's arm, restraining her. "I have always done my duty. Regardless of what you think, Iegani, I am a good queen. Someday, I will be a great queen. You need only stay alive long enough to witness it."

Maura saw her sword and dagger on a table and went over to gather them. She turned and faced Iegani squarely. "I am ready," she said with finality.

There was a gleam of triumph in Iegani's eyes. He summoned Tarsus and Toppo.

They hurried into the room carrying a golden sedan with carved outstretched wings attached to two long poles. Bowing low, they glanced at Maura and sensed great hostility coming from her.

Iegani motioned to the chair. "They will carry you to the Mother Bogazkoy. Empress Gitar and I will follow to witness the union."

Saying nothing, Maura lowered herself into the portable throne. She signaled to Toppo and Tarsus with a nod of her head.

Grasping the poles, they lifted the chair and hurried out of the room, running into a massive hallway made of stone blocks where hundreds of Dinii stood pressed close to the walls like statues.

At the end of the hallway was a pair of the largest carved doors that Maura had ever seen. They must have stood sixty feet high. The mammoth doors were slowly swung open by Dinii pulling on large ropes looped through holes in the handle design.

Toppo and Tarsus ran toward the door as it was opening and flew out into the sky with Maura sitting in the golden chair.

She turned to look at the doors again. She could see little as Gitar and Iegani were following close behind with the rest of the Dinii contingent.

Turning forward in her seat, Maura gazed upon the Forbidden City of Atetelco, the long-lost capital of the Overlords of Kaseri.

Gigantic buildings mounted on marble and granite pillars stood everywhere. The main floor of each building stood at least forty feet off the ground. Each building had one main entrance, but Maura could see neither windows nor other exits in any of the structures. The buildings vaguely reminded her of descriptions from scrolls brought from the House of Magi.

Maura strained her eyes to see everything. Some

buildings possessed no walls, just a roof. Maura guessed these structures had been open-air markets. Below were overgrown gardens and remnants of pathways. Creeping vines covered most of the Dinii statues spotting the grounds of the city.

Camping underneath many of the buildings or in the gardens were Hasan Daegian soldiers from the western division of her army. Tents and cooking fires were strewn all across the eastern side of the city along with laundry hanging from makeshift clotheslines.

Maura was startled to see shirts and diapers flapping in the breeze. Then she realized the Dinii were housing not only her army but also the western Hasan Daegian population.

Atetelco had become a refugee camp. Many of the buildings her people were lodged in had ropes and ladders hanging from the first-floor entrance. Women scurried up a ladder or pulled some heavy object up on a rope. Others, living on the ground, were putting out their campfires and tearing down their tents. Soldiers were lining up in combat formation.

Maura peered closer. *They are getting ready for battle!* she thought. She strained to look beyond the eastern part of the city. In the distance, a thin line of dust could be seen approaching the city. DORAK IS COMING WITH HIS ARMY!

Maura waved to catch Toppo's attention. Cupping her hands to her mouth, Maura yelled, "Fly lower around my soldiers. They must see me."

Toppo signaled to Tarsus, and they descended near the busy Hasan Daegian soldiers.

Looking up at the approaching Dinii, many of the Hasan Daegians did not recognize their queen. Maura straightened herself in the golden sedan and tried to look every inch a sovereign worthy of them. She waved and called, cheering them on to victory. Slowly, the people acknowledged her.

The Hasan Daegians, depressed from months of deprivation and isolation in the Forbidden Zone, took heart when they saw Maura waving to them. She looked well and strong. As her manner gave them hope, they cheered and clapped each other on the back. Others danced little jigs, so happy were they to see her.

Receiving a reproach telepathically from Iegani, Toppo finally veered the chair away and headed toward the very western part of the city near the sea.

Maura looked behind.

Iegani and Gitar followed with many Dinii warriors in tow. The rest of the Dinii stayed with the Hasan Daegians to fight Dorak's steadily encroaching army.

They descended toward an inlet between the shore and a tiny island. Deserted boardwalks, dilapidated docks, and empty storehouses along the shore of the city gave testimony that the Dinii had once been a potent force at sea as well as on land.

Maura still could not get used to the size of the buildings, all of which were built several stories off the ground. She wondered if the Dinii had once been a taller race of beings as the entrances to the building were immense.

She thought about the City of the Peaks, which had existed on the highest mountain in Hasan Daeg. Though adequate for a Dini's needs, the stick and stone buildings possessed none of the architectural wonders with sculptures and mosaics that she witnessed in the Forbidden City. She did not have long to ponder as Toppo and Tarsus began guiding the chair precariously through streets and finally onto one of the docks. They gently laid the sedan down.

"Are you well?" Toppo asked with great concern.

Maura reassured her with a quick nod.

Tarsus helped Maura out of the chair and held her while she tried to steady her shaking legs.

"I much prefer the solid back of a Dini to that of a golden throne that might fall apart," said Maura, holding onto Tarsus' hands.

He snorted his approval.

Maura found her land legs and looked at Tarsus.

"Now what?"

Toppo answered her. "It is only a little further." She pointed to a small cliff with steps carved near the bottom leading to the sea. "You must climb down this cliff to the stairs. Follow the stairs to the sea. There will be ten more steps underwater. At the bottom of these steps is a small tunnel, which you must swim through. You will come up into a rock chamber. Follow the hallway from the chamber, and you will eventually come to the Mother."

"What about you?" asked Maura, shivering in the sea breeze.

"We have to dive from another angle to gather enough momentum to swim under the sea." Toppo pointed to her feathers. "Did you forget they are water repellent?"

Tarsus and Toppo murmured, "Good luck," and bowed low. They spread their wings and flew high into the sky where Iegani and Gitar hovered as well as the Dinii warriors following them.

Maura tied back her black hair with a leather thong torn from her clothes. Securing her dagger, she climbed down until she reached the slick steps. Once she came to the bottom step, she tentatively stuck her foot into the water. Feeling the icy cold through her leather boots, she placed her hand over her womb. Maura closed her eyes and calmed herself. "Baby," she whispered to her unborn child, "if you want to live, stay strong." She gently patted her stomach. Taking a deep breath, Maura plunged into the green water. The shock of the water's cold forced the air out of her lungs, but she managed to acclimate herself. Losing the outline of the steps, she came back up for air and found the first step in the water. Taking another deep breath, she dove underneath again, this time taking care to follow the outline of the steps.

Maura counted carefully and swiftly followed the steps down to the tenth one. There she felt for an opening and found the small tunnel. She entered it quickly as she was running out of air, and her lungs were burning.

Hearing a crashing noise behind her, Maura realized the Dinii had entered the water. This encouraged her to keep going. Ahead, she saw light streaming through the water and swam toward it until her head popped out in a small opening. Maura grabbed the sides, trying to pull up, but coughing and spewing water so hard she fell back. Again, she struggled and managed to dig her heels into the side of the tunnel's slick wall, finally pulling herself onto a marble floor. Hearing commotion, she leaned down into the water's opening. Seeing feathers, she reached down into the dark water and, grabbing a fistful of them, pulled Toppo toward her.

Toppo grabbed the side of the hole and hoisted herself into the chamber. "I almost couldn't get through," she wheezed. "The tunnel is so small!" Catching her breath, she leaned down and helped Maura look for more struggling Dinii.

Seeing the outline of the royal black and white feathers, Toppo submerged her torso into the icy water and hauled a gagging Gitar out. Gitar stumbled into a corner to catch her breath.

Tarsus emerged from the tunnel hole without any assistance as did Iegani. As males, they were both smaller and were not as distressed. Spreading their wings, they shook themselves off with vigor.

Yeti and Benzar emerged, followed by the rest of the Dinii.

Maura backed off to get out of the way of the water spray. She was shivering and rubbed the goosebumps on her arms and legs vigorously. Once her teeth stopped chattering, Maura checked her dagger. Then she explored the chamber.

It was a natural cave, but the floor was enhanced with rare green and white marble. Delicate reliefs had been carved into the walls by superb artists.

Maura went over to them. Tracing their outlines with her fingertips, she studied the reliefs closely. There were carvings of past Dinii empresses pinning down beings of strange-looking races with their taloned feet. Some of the empresses looked as though they were about to tear off their captives' heads.

Beside each relief, there were lines of pictographs. Maura recognized many of the symbols. "Look here!" she said excitedly. "These marks are ancient Anqarian!"

Toppo and Tarsus joined her at the wall and examined the carvings.

Iegani and Gitar glanced at each other.

Standing behind, Iegani reminded Maura. "The Mother Bogazkoy awaits." He helped a reluctant Gitar to her feet. "Down this way," he said, pointing to an ancient passageway that led from the chamber.

Maura peered down the passageway. "I won't be able to see in the dark."

"Follow me," said Iegani. "I have visited the Mother Bogazkoy many times since coming here. She is anxious for you."

"I know what the Bogazkoy is. The Lahorian, Rakel, told me about it."

"Rakel only told you part of it, I am sure," replied Iegani. He started to explain when a green light suddenly flashed through the tunnel opening into the room. Malevolent looking fingers of light crept about the floor as though searching.

Gitar wailed, "The Black Cacodemon. He has found us!"

Not losing a moment, Iegani grabbed Maura's hand and began racing down a corridor.

Maura stumbled and fell in the dark but felt Iegani's hands drag her to her feet. Looking back, she could make out Gitar and the rest of the Dinii running behind her.

"Keep going," Gitar mouthed, her eyes wide with fright Maura hardened her resolve and began running as quickly as Iegani. Realizing she was keeping pace with him, Iegani let go of Maura's hand and concentrated on taking the correct passageway in the myriad of honey-combed corridors. Like the underground pathways in the royal Hasan Daegian palace, the corridor on the left was always the one taken.

Glancing back, Maura could see the faint glow of a pulsating light in the hallway. A terrible boom sounded in the passageway, shaking the walls about them. The Black Cacodemon was getting closer.

Iegani took one last left turn, and Maura followed him into an open chamber. He stopped suddenly.

Maura followed suit and looked about. She was in the chamber of the Mother Bogazkoy. As she expected, it was almost identical to the chamber of the Royal Bogazkoy in the Hasan Daegian palace, except there was no boat. Across a rolling lake of seawater was a small rock island on which abided the Mother Bogazkoy.

Making out a small blue lump on the rock, Maura turned toward Iegani. "Surely that small thing can't be the Mother?"

As soon as Maura spoke, the Mother Bogazkoy unfurled its magnificent leaves from the tight ball it slept in. A robust blue-green trunk emerged from the rocks with long green tendrils, which unfurled into the water.

"I hear the voice of my beloved's child," sang a melodious voice that was neither male nor female. Tendrils emerged from the water and quickly crept around Maura's body before she had time to move. "Centuries ago, your ancestor Rosalind came to me and helped to rejuvenate my kind. I would have been lost without her. Since then I have pledged myself only to her offspring and, in return, have given them my precious gifts of health and long life, small tokens of my esteem. Be my love now. Come to me."

Maura pushed away a probing tendril. "I am with child. I will not help you if you harm my baby," she shouted, amazed that the plant was sentient and could communicate.

The tendril stopped moving about Maura and loosened its grip on her.

Gitar and Iegani held their breaths.

The Mother Bogazkoy spoke after a long pause. "Your joy is my joy. Blessed is this union of human love. I will give your offspring the greatest gift of all. Everlasting life!"

"Everlasting? That is a curse, not a blessing," Maura argued.

A great pounding sounded in the hallway.

Realizing she did not have any more time, Maura dove into the hot salt water and swam for the Mother.

Tendrils gathered around Maura's waist while others entered the water. Together the tendrils lifted her out of the steaming lake and onto the rock home of the Mother Bogazkoy.

Without hesitation, Maura pulled herself up by the Bogazkoy's tendrils and hurried to the trunk of the plant. Fine hair covered the trunk of the plant, which now looked almost like skin.

"You are my beloved mate. I will not hurt you. You will know ecstasy with me. From your body, I will extract the eggs I need. My issue will replace me as I am getting old." The Mother's voice seemed to come from every direction at once.

"The Royal Bogazkoy never produced an offspring."

"Only I have that capacity, but now my long life is nearly spent. I must provide an heir to take my place."

"If the Royal Bogazkoy did not need to reproduce, why did it allow only one royal child?"

"Its gift to the queens was too powerful. It is the pact Rosalind made with me. In exchange for long life and power, only one child to each ruler. A second child could be born, but only under special circumstances. The secret had to be kept and not abused."

Maura placed her hand on her stomach. "Save my child."

The Mother Bogazkoy assured, "The baby will not be harmed if you do as I say. Move not unless I move you. Resist not and I will go nowhere near the child. Move and I cannot be responsible. Simply yield unto me. Do you understand, my love?"

A great crash sounded across the lake, but Maura did not look. She realized what had happened.

The Black Cacodemon had gotten through and was now in the chamber. Wide strobes of green, purplish light flashed on the walls as did long beams of a bluish white.

Maura threw herself at the center of the Mother Bogazkoy and immediately limbs from the base of the trunk rose and encased her. For a moment, Maura struggled as she heard her clothes slashed by sharp tips of the tendrils and thought for a moment that she might suffocate in the tight encasement, but relaxed as the plant sprayed a soothing mist near her face. Her body became limp as she felt its limbs tighten on her skin. Inhaling the mist deeply, she found herself aroused. She did not protest as small leathery tips emerging from the side of the branches began probing her orifices. Maura welcomed their intrusion into her body. The memory of the Royal Bogazkoy shot through her mind, and Maura gave herself willingly to the plant.

She felt her legs pulled apart as several probes gently entered her anus, urethra, and finally, her vagina. Maura lifted her buttocks to help the probes until she heard the Bogazkoy remind her not to move. Her bottom felt wet and slippery. The living tissue of the probes issued a jet of mucus-like sap that lubricated her orifices and coated her skin. It even lubricated her tear ducts as the branches spread their tendrils across her face and entered her ears, eyes, and nose.

Maura forgot about the pleasure of the Bogazkoy as the tendrils merged to become a blue mask on her face, finally entering her mouth. Maura resisted, but the branches issued another cloud of mist, and she immediately sank into a stupor of intense physical pleasure.

Feeling her lips open, something sweet pried Maura's teeth apart only to wiggle down her throat. Being stroked and tweaked in every conceivable manner, Maura abandoned herself to the touch of the

Bogazkoy. Her nipples and womanhood were rubbed and pulled upon until she was not able to contain herself. She arched her back and heard herself cry out in culmination. The probes in her anus and vagina intensified their manipulation as one tiny probe found her left ovary and injected a hollow tube into its fleshy sack to suck out tiny eggs.

Feeling a sharp pain in her abdomen, Maura squirmed and began to gag. The entire encasement of tendrils raised tiny needle-like hairs, pricking the skin on her body. A blue substance spurted into her skin and bloodstream. Maura felt her bowels loosen as the small jets of blue liquid shot into her veins. Now she could feel the eggs in her other ovary taken as her heart pumped faster, and flashes of blue and yellow light exploded in her head causing her to momentarily lose consciousness.

Then it was all over.

Instinctively, Maura knew the mating was completed. The Mother Bogazkoy had what it wanted from her. Slowly the tendrils began to withdraw, leaving Maura covered with a glistening blue slime and her own wastes. She felt the tendrils of the Mother Bogazkoy help her sit up as it massaged her forehead and neck.

Maura slowly opened her eyes. At first, she was so dazed, she could not comprehend the chaos in the room. As soon as her head cleared, she reached for her belly.

She gasped. Her hands and belly were dark. She rubbed her skin with her fingers. Standing, she checked the rest of her body. Her skin was ebony, but not the ebony of night as she first had thought, but rather the black of the darkest blue and rich with the power of the Bogazkoy. Only the nails on her toes and fingers appeared pale.

"Maura, help us!" came a cry from across the water.

Maura's head snapped up as her eyes scanned the chamber.

A wounded Toppo was trying to drag the unconscious body of Gitar behind a boulder out of harm's way.

Yeti, Tarsus, and Iegani plus many other Dinii were forming a barrier before Gitar.

The Black Cacodemon stalked back and forth in front of the Dinii. His cowl was pulled back, exposing a pale, enlarged head with tired wisps of hair straggling about his ears. The top of the Cacodemon's head was misshapen and bent with red, ugly scars running down the back of his skull as though something had struck his head many times. Magical incantations were tattooed on the scars.

Believing her end was at hand, Toppo screamed and

flung herself over Gitar.

From behind the Black Cacodemon, a battered Tarsus threw himself at the wizard but bounced off an energy field.

As the light from his hands grew stronger, the Black Cacodemon's eyes took on a gleam that was akin to madness. He let out a sharp little bark.

Seeing her friends harmed, Maura threw her hands in front of her and cried out, "STOP!"

The Black Cacodemon diverted his eyes and stared at the Hasan Daegian queen standing defiantly in front of the Mother Bogazkoy whose tendrils waved in an agitated manner. His eyes narrowed as he took in the filthy, soiled woman standing naked before his power.

"I'm going to kill your silly friends, and then I'm going to come after you," he taunted, envious of the gift of the Mother Bogazkoy.

"Or maybe I should kill you first," he spat out, thrusting his hand into the air.

A bolt of ugly drab green light shot at Maura. She ducked while holding her arms before her face. She felt a strong sensation like wind surround her and then dissipate. Surprised that she was not hurt, she looked questioningly at the Mother Bogazkoy.

The Mother Bogazkoy had tucked its branches near the base of the trunk.

Maura could hear the plant hissing with anger. "We are one?"

"Yes," replied the Mother Bogazkoy. "You now have the strength of a hundred Dinii. He wishes to drink of my sap, my lifeblood. Feel your power. He wants what you have. Kill him before he destroys us both."

The Black Cacodemon forgot about the Dinii. He exhaled a gaseous cloud, which drifted about his feet. Stepping on the cloud, he floated across the water toward Maura and the Bogazkoy.

The wizard's excitement at being so close to the Mother Bogazkoy was barely contained. He had searched the world over for it. He had killed, schemed, and endured patiently for this very moment. The Black Cacodemon's eyes were wide with anticipation and desire for the gift of a long and healthy life.

A tendril of the Mother Bogazkoy waved wildly.

Maura could sense the plant feared the Black Cacodemon as she did. Maura ran to her scraps of clothing and searched through the pile trying to find her dagger. Sighting it, she grabbed it quickly and ran to the edge of the rock, determined to stop the sorcerer from stepping upon it.

The Mother Bogazkoy slipped several tendrils into the water in the hopes of pulling him down into the water, but to no avail.

The protective field surrounding the Cacodemon was too strong.

The Mother Bogazkoy withdrew its tendrils, wrapping its trunk tightly, and sank into a rock crevice, leaving Maura to do what she could.

The Black Cacodemon reached the base of the rock.

Maura moved to intercept the magician, but he merely waved his hand, throwing her out of the way.

Angry, the Mother Bogazkoy emerged halfway out of the rock crevice and faced the Black Cacodemon. "Do not hurt my beloved!" the Bogazkoy demanded, trembling with rage.

The Black Cacodemon merely shrugged. "Give me what I want, and I will leave in peace, hurting no one else."

"What would that be?" asked the Bogazkoy in its strange hissing voice.

"The same as she," the wizard whispered, pointing to Maura. "Immortality, life, health, invincibility."

"I don't understand," the Bogazkoy lied, hoping for more time.

The Black Cacodemon raised his hand and shot another thunderbolt at Maura. She raised her arms, covering her face as before and was spared the worst of the blow, but still was shaken.

"STOP AT ONCE!" shouted an angry voice from across the water.

Both the Black Cacodemon and Maura turned.

"Dorak!" Maura cried.

From beneath his bronze visor, Dorak's eyes took in his wife. He was shocked by her filthy, naked appearance. Her hair was long and disheveled and hung in great tangled mats. Her skin was black and glistened from the strange glow of the lake. Yet she stood defiant and proud before the Black Cacodemon.

The Black Cacodemon smiled painfully. "Dorak, I'm so glad you are here at last." He pointed to Maura. "She reached the Bogazkoy before I could."

As the wizard faced Dorak, Maura began inching her way toward him with her dagger hidden behind her back.

Dorak scanned the scorch marks on the rock walls and the bleeding Dinii, who were breathing heavily, but watching him with steady eyes. He recognized the black and white feathers of one of the Dinii, whose tips were dyed with purple as the sign of royalty. He bowed. "Empress Gitar, we seem destined to meet under the most insidious circumstances possible."

Dorak reached down and, placing his hands under her arms, lifted Gitar up and leaned her against a wall. He was amazed at how heavy she was. For just a second he wondered how she could fly so gracefully.

"Thank you, Dorak. Now, if only you had been this considerate at the City of the Peaks," Gitar said, struggling for breath. She placed her hand upon her chest as her eyelids fluttered.

Dorak saw that she was bleeding from the side of her head and hoped she would faint, sparing her any more pain or discomfort. He raised the visor on his helmet. "War is war, Madam. It was nothing personal."

"Ah, that is where you are wrong, Aga Dorak. The loss of my daughters and my home is very personal."

Dorak's lips pressed into a thin line. He said nothing but turned toward his wizard who was waving his hand to attack. "Don't do it, Zedek Sadjin!"

The Black Cacodemon gasped in surprise. "How do you know my name?"

"I know many things about you, spellweaver. I know centuries ago you were a mere stable boy until the magician Knoxel took you as an apprentice. You served him for twenty-two years until you stole all of his secrets and then murdered him."

The Black Cacodemon held his hands up beseechingly. "Dorak, we had a pact. This girl can give us what we want. She can give you the power you've always dreamed of."

"It is very tempting, but I have decided to change

our little deal."

"How did you get into the city?" Maura asked of Dorak.

"With a very large army that I hope is, at this moment, cutting yours to pieces," answered Dorak, watching the Black Cacodemon. "So it would be to your army's benefit if you joined me and together we both tell them to cease."

Maura laughed. "Do you think I endured these hardships to listen to your lies?" she asked, slowly inching her way closer to the Black Cacodemon. "How could you move your army so quickly?"

Dorak removed his chain mail gloves. "He's not the only one who knows a little magic," said Dorak, wagging his thumb toward the Black Cacodemon. "I'm willing to forgive and forget as you must."

"I know why you want me. You want to kill me and secure the power of the Mother Bogazkoy for yourself."

"Just what is this power? This maggot of a man has manipulated armies and kings to get to this smelly cave where that hideous blue plant lives. All for what?" Dorak demanded.

"For invincibility," Maura rasped.

"You see! I have not lied about the power of the Bogazkoy," cried the Black Cacodemon. He pointed at Maura. "She knows!"

"Shut up. No one was speaking to you," snarled Dorak, raising his sword in irritation. He began pacing back and forth, trying to decide what to do. He would have to wait for the rest of his men so they could make a raft and go over to get both Maura and the Black Cacodemon.

The Black Cacodemon, seeing Dorak's attention diverted, threw a green ball of fire at him.

"Dorak, watch out!" cried Maura as she jumped at the Black Cacodemon. She was thrown back, but Maura focused her mind and sprang at him again. She had power now. She had to believe in herself. This time she penetrated his swirling aura and stabbed him in the side.

The Black Cacodemon twisted in pain. His black eyes had no bottom, like the blackest tempest.

Maura struck again, sinking the dagger deep into his bosom.

The wizard howled as he clutched his medallion.

But Maura tore the medallion from his neck and struck again at his chest. As he yielded to his death, the Black Cacodemon fell to his knees, grabbing Maura's legs. She shook his clammy hands off and kicked him for good measure. He looked at the Hasan Daegian queen standing defiantly over him one last time, opened his mouth to weave a spell before falling into a quiet death.

Maura looked across the water. She had not been quick enough.

Dorak had been hit and was lying very still. There was the look of death about him.

Feeling her heart shudder, Maura dove into the water and, after a minute's swimming, pulled herself onto the other shore. She groaned.

There was neither Dorak nor any of the Dinii.

Flipping her dripping hair back from her eyes, Maura rose haphazardly from her knees and made her way to the corridor.

No blood or water spotted the floor. Returning to the Mother Bogazkoy's chamber, she examined the walls and floor for another way out. She dove into the water and searched the bottom, thinking they had tried to get across and perished in the water. There was no sign of them.

Hours upon hours, she searched. Up and down the corridors she went, calling their names, looking for a sign of the Dinii and her husband. Finally, having exhausted all possibilities, she admitted defeat before the Mother Bogazkoy, which hummed sympathetically and let loose a terrible, lonely cry.

The Black Cacodemon must have uttered a spell before he died while she stood in false triumph over him. The spell banished her companions and the man she loved, leaving only his sword.

Maura fell to her knees and beat her breast in a steady rhythm as she wailed the death chant for her lost love and friends. For a few brief moments, she went mad with blinding grief.

Weaving down the stone hallways, Maura called out Dorak's name until she felt as though she was a mere shadow thrown upon the walls. She felt herself become smaller and fainter in her mind.

Finding herself in the entrance chamber again, she fell to the floor and clutched her arms about her. She was alone in the world. Even Dorak was no more. The Dinii were gone. Her family was destroyed. At the realization of her terrible aloneness and the numbing pain of her despair, Maura's mind went quiet and finally blackened into nothingness.

A cold draft blew through the halls of the Mother Bogazkoy's chamber. An unseen hand gently pushed the hair out of Maura's eyes and silently murmured her name, "Maura. Maura. Listen to the secret. Find me. Play the song for me. I've been waiting all these years for you. Play the song."

Maura opened her eyes, catching her reflection in the polished marble. The front lock of her black hair was streaked with grey, and there were grim lines about her mouth. She gently touched her battered face with stained, grimy hands.

"Who are you?" she whispered. "You are not the sweet girl who wanted to marry the dashing Chaun Maaun. He will not even see you now. You are not the consort of Dorak, Aga of Bhuttan. He is gone, and you will never know if he ever really loved you. The answer to that riddle will forever haunt you. There is no one left. I alone know the secret of the Bogazkoy." She bent forward and kissed the lips of her countenance in the marble reflection. Clumsily, she pulled herself up and searched the passages until she came to a relief carving of the uultepes.

Play the song, thought Maura. *Were the symbols on her back musical notes and not words?*

Maura tapped the symbols carved into the torsos of the uultepes as portrayed on her tattoo. Musical sounds emitted from the carvings similar to that of a lyre.

Maura stood away from the wall.

Slowly, the figures of the uultepes changed color until they were a dark red, causing their outlines to glimmer. Brighter and brighter, the uultepes glowed as the wall shook and rumbled. The outlines of the uultepes rippled as though unseen muscles were awakening from millennia of sleep. Growling, two uultepes stepped off the carved wall and stood before Maura in flesh, bone, and sinew. They positioned themselves on either side of the Hasan Daegian queen never to leave again so long as Maura lived.

The carved walls continued rumbling until one part of the wall pulled apart from the other, leaving a secret chamber exposed. There stood an ancient throne surrounded by rusted swords and dull shields. Large trunks stood everywhere, filled with fading parchments, mold-covered scrolls, and locked caskets.

On the throne sat a collapsed skeleton. A golden crown was haphazardly resting on its side by the skull, which lay on the throne's seat while bits of bone from the hands along with the feet were strewn across the dusty floor.

Maura went to the skeleton, searching among the dust pile. After several moments of brushing aside bone fragments, she finally cried out in triumph. In the crumbled remains of Rosalind, Maura found an ancient gold ring with the seal of the Overlords of Kaseri upon it. It was the ring given by the Dinii to Rosalind, the first queen of Hasan Daeg and lover of the Mother Bogazkoy.

Laughing, Maura kicked away the rest of the skeleton, which landed upon the steps of the ivory and marble throne. The large uultepes took their places beside the throne. One began licking its matted fur. The other lay down and closed its eyes, seemingly at rest.

Hearing a disturbance of the water beyond the chamber, Maura rested Dorak's sword on her lap and faced the entrance with her arms akimbo.

She knew Dorak's men were coming. Using her hair, she wiped away her tears as she waited to meet them. Pulling her grief deep inside, she assumed a mask of power and arrogance.

Her naked black-blue skin began to glow as she felt the power of the Mother Bogazkoy pulsate within her. She did not fear Dorak's men. They would see what she wanted them to see, and she would remain the Bhuttanian Empress as she carried the aga's child.

But more than that, Maura had the golden seal of the Overlords. She was now the most powerful being on Kaseri.

Regent Empress Maura de Magela, Aganess of the Bhuttanian Empire, Tenth Queen of Hasan Daeg and Great Mother of Kaseri had a world to govern. After all she had endured, one thing she learned was that one takes power. It is not given.

She was born to rule.

And Maura intended to rule the Bhuttanian Empire.

Wall Of Conquest
The Princess Maura Tales IV
Abigail Keam

1

Empress Maura de Magela looked unhappy.

This pleased Timon not one bit, but he could say nothing until his master, the Consul Rubank, whose palanquin he trudged alongside, beckoned.

The empress tapped her fingers impatiently on the arm of her carved throne made from bones of those vanquished by previous Bhuttanian rulers—and by her as well. The empress had anyone who opposed her leadership executed, including Hasan Daegians.

The throne sat upon a carved wooden dais, decorated with Imperial flags and resting upon a painted wagon pulled by a team of festive borax wearing plumed headgear. A detachable canopy of rare wood carved with images of dragons and other Bhuttanian symbols covered the rolling platform.

One had to be alert not to stumble and be crushed under the wagon for it could not stop in haste.

The empress motioned to halt.

Soldiers rushed and unhooked the wagon from the plodding borax. This was the quickest way to pause the wagon as the borax would continue moving until the lead bull was coaxed to turn.

Timon, who acted as Rubank's scribe, kneeled as did others.

Fanning herself, the empress stepped down onto the dusty ground.

The young scribe did not like having close contact with the empress. She frightened him with her blue skin and fierce expressions. Her mercurial moods were such that he always waited for a calamity to fall. Timon wished he had remained a nameless scribe in the guild for he despised his duties as royal scribe, but Rubank had handpicked him.

If Empress Maura noticed Timon's discomfort, she did not show it.

They were on their way to Bhuttan so she could officially assume the reins of government in the capital city of Bhuttani. She was the mother of Princess Dyanna, heir to the throne of the Bhuttanian Empire, and would rule as Dowager Regent until the child became of age.

Timon chuckled when he thought of the empress relinquishing power she had ruthlessly fought to gain. He doubted she would voluntarily turn over control when the time came for the child to ascend to the throne.

Get out your tablets, commanded Rubank with the sign language Timon had devised for the consul to communicate with him.

Previously, Timon had to guess what the consul wanted or wait for him to write his instructions down. Timon's thoughts that a tongueless advisor to a ruler benefited no one and Rubank was too old to be of any real use were kept to himself.

How many times do I have to tell you that you must be ready for the empress at all times! Rubank loved his new way of communicating and was quite adept at it.

Timon shook his head. He regretted that he had designed the hand language, for Rubank never shut up now.

As Timon unwrapped moist clay tablets from his leather pouch, two uultepes jumped off the royal platform with singular grace. The great beasts, conjured by magic, constantly stayed near the side of the empress. One pressed close to Timon, knocking him down. It circled, taking care to look Timon in the eye.

The strong odor of the brindle animals mingled with

the dust of the marching army caused Timon to erupt in a fit of coughing. He brought his fist to his mouth, hoping to stifle the hack rising from his chest. He glanced up red-faced to see if the empress had noticed his breach of protocol.

She had not.

Timon immediately stood up, and grabbed his tablet and stylus, ignoring the snickers of the guards, who watched as the uultepes circled again pressing even closer. Timon, ready this time, took the sharp end of his wooden stylus and stabbed a paw of one of the giant cats.

The uultepe's eyes widened. Angry, it trotted toward its mistress after giving Timon a malevolent glance.

Timon smiled. Brushing off his dusty knees with several quiet groans, he reluctantly followed. Timon made a mental note to speak to Rubank about a transfer again as he stumbled along. Fumbling with his stylus and wet clay tablets, he dodged an army trudging in the opposite direction.

Scribes used beeswax, wood, and cloth, but clay tablets were preferred on a military march. The wet clay was never allowed to dry out and could be used over and over again.

Timon thought the heavy clay tablets a nuisance and hated working with them, but then Timon hated everything about his life at the moment. Oh, he longed to escape.

Empress Maura strode steadily toward the rear of the army with her hands clasped behind her back.

Two lads-in-waiting struggled to keep the costly embroidered train of her light blue and gold gown out of the dirt.

Underneath the skirt of her gown, Timon could see leather boots and heavy, twined cotton pants commonly worn by most Bhuttanian soldiers. He was sure there would also be a dagger or two tucked away somewhere on her royal personage.

Timon was aware the empress only donned the beautiful gown to please the more conservative elements of her court. She wore the soldier's clothes to please herself. On a second's notice, she could rip the gown off, becoming a skilled combatant. She had become the deadliest woman in the Bhuttanian Empire whom no one could best, regardless of their proficiency with weapons.

There were others who were more dexterous in swinging an axe or lighter on their feet with a sword, but she possessed brute strength and lightning fast agility.

Perhaps a Dini possessed sufficient skill and strength to topple the empress, but the Dinii were seen no more.

The empress rested her eyes upon Timon, as she inclined her head. "What is the name of you, boy?"

Timon blinked and heard himself replying, "My name is Timon Ben Ibin Moab. My people are from the Steppes of Moab named after the first of my ancestors." He bowed his head.

"We will cut through the Steppes of Moab before we reach Bhuttani."

Timon continued to stare at the ground. "Yes, Empress. My home is only a week or so from here."

"You have been in the consul's employment for how long?"

"Many moons."

He's unusually clever, Great Mother, Rubank wrote on a tablet for the empress. *He has a talent for symbols and language.*

Maura considered this information for a moment after reading the tablet. "He must be, Consul, as I do not see your usual interpreters with you."

She addressed Timon directly. "Timon Ben Ibin Moab, you will come to my tent after the evening meal and show me from whence you came on my map," commanded the empress. She turned her head from the consul and the lowly scribe, who realized he had just wet himself.

Luckily, Timon's long woven tunic covered his disgrace. He touched his fingers to his heart and then his lips with a theatrical flourish. Seeing Rubank was displeased, Timon gave the usual Bhuttanian salute of the fist to his heart. With a wave of her hand, Maura dismissed both Rubank and Timon.

Timon reluctantly followed the silent Rubank and helped him into his palanquin. The years of war between the Bhuttanians and Hasan Daegians had strained the royal consul's heart. Rubank did little these days to be of real use to the empress except give her occasional advice.

Still, the empress showed Rubank respect by letting him keep his title and honors. In fact, Timon noticed she rarely let Rubank out of her sight.

Timon pinched the side of his face. *It is regarding things, which are none of my business that got me noticed by the empress today!* thought Timon, but still he pondered the reasons why Maura de Magela, Dowager Regent, Aganess of the Bhuttanian Empire, Tenth Queen of Hasan Daeg, and Great Mother of Kaseri, might need an old man who was past his prime.

Timon had heard Rubank served Queen Abisola, Maura's mother, for much of her reign. *That would make him—let's see—past one hundred, maybe older,* Timon thought as he counted on his fingers. Timon shook his head in disbelief and hurried to catch up with Rubank's palanquin.

These Hasan Daegians lived a very long time.

2

The army followed the same routine.

Before dusk, the empress had her husband's favorite horse saddled and brought to her. With the uultepes for company, she rode behind the main body of the army where she awaited scouts, who had been searching for stray feathers that might have fallen from the elusive Dinii.

Upon their return each day, she'd excitedly go through their pouches full of feathers with eager anticipation until she dropped the last feather in disappointment at finding no Dini feather.

"Maybe tomorrow," she murmured to the sweating couriers. "Go. Get something to eat." Empress Maura would then gaze at the distant horizon until darkness.

Timon was so bored with this daily scene, he thought he'd scream. To ease his frustration, he played games in his imagination, waiting for the empress to return to her wagon.

Sometimes, he looked at Rubank, imagining him dressed as a fool, complete with a purple face and a green nose. This would cause Timon to smile. Other times, he pictured the empress on her knees begging him to make love to her.

"Timon, why are you grinning?"

Timon's eyes widened as he realized the empress was standing before him speaking.

"Are you dim-witted?"

"No, Great Mother. My mind drifted off. A hundred pardons."

Maura's eyes narrowed as her jaw tightened. "That could be a foolish mistake, which might cost you your life, Royal Scribe."

Timon's face flushed. He bowed very low. "A thousand pardons. It will never happen again."

"I'm not talking about me causing you harm, boy. An assassin could make straight for me, and if you are not alert, you could fall right in her pathway. Death by mere association. Beware!" Grumbling to herself about Timon, the somber empress strode off on foot in haste.

One of the uultepes turned and snarled a warning before following her queen.

Timon mouthed an oath under his breath at the

uultepe. Struggling to hold his tablets and writing sticks, Timon hurried after the empress, dropping a stylus here and there.

Maura made way to her tent, which was hurriedly being prepared by many servants. Out of the corner of her eye, Maura saw flickering lights on the northern horizon as eventide approached.

No troops of hers were straggling in from that direction.

Maura speculated on who it might be and wondered how her scouts had failed to inform her of approaching strangers in the area.

All the local people had given their fealty to her, so she knew it was not an opposing force. "You there," she called to a Bhuttanian. "Help this boy up."

The soldier immediately ran over to Timon and intertwined his hands together. Timon clumsily swung a foot in the soldier's hands and climbed atop his shoulders, straining to get a look at the entourage approaching the army.

"What do you see?" called Maura.

"They ride Bhuttanian war steeds. There are numerous wagons as well, so there must be women and children, but their banners are too far away. I can't make them out." Timon jumped down with his pens spilling upon the ground. He thanked the embarrassed soldier helping to pick them up.

"Let's hurry to my tent. A courier awaits with news, I'm sure," she called to Timon.

"I hope so, or it will be someone's head," muttered Timon, breaking into a run.

As expected, an out-of-breath courier waited in the tent as the empress strode in.

"Is it an emergency?" she asked the courier.

The stalwart courier shook her head, struggling to regain her breath.

Maura smiled. "Good. You may tell me as I make ready for dinner."

The courier followed the empress into her private quarters.

Lads-in-waiting stood eagerly.

Maura washed her grimy face and hands. Grabbing a towel, she sat as one of her servants pulled off her boots and washed her feet. "What news do you have, woman?" Maura grunted as one of the servants tried to coax her unruly hair into a braid.

"Prince KiKu of Hittal humbly requests permission to enter the perimeter of Her Majesty's camp."

Timon shivered when he heard the name KiKu.

"KiKu! Here?" asked Maura as she reached back, grabbing the annoying comb out of the servant's hand and hurling it across the room.

Maura stood, and two servants immediately began unbuckling her pants and shirt. A beautiful pale green lounging gown with gold trousers was produced for her inspection. Pleased with the embroidered flower designs on the gown, she nodded yes. The empress stood with her arms extended. The servants removed her tunic and wiped down her arms, chest, and back. Stepping out of her trousers, Maura's legs and buttocks were cleansed as well.

The lads, delighted the empress approved their selection, dressed her.

The courier stood at attention and stared at the tent wall, never looking at the empress.

Sensing the courier was embarrassed at being in the presence of the empress while dressing, Maura gave leave for the courier to retire.

Relieved, the courier backed out of the chamber while bowing.

Maura turned to Timon, who was kneeling in obeisance with his forehead pressed against a carpeted floor. "Ask Prince KiKu to join me for dinner this evening. Tonight, he will set his tents outside the perimeter, but tomorrow, he may place his tent next to mine."

Timon was about to remind the empress that his guild only allowed him to write messages, not deliver them but thought better of it. He rose to his feet and bowed.

"Be early for dinner to take notes and work with my map," Maura ordered sharply as she rotated on her stool to face the blushing Bhuttanian.

Timon salaamed and backed out of the chamber. Once outside, Timon grimaced as he pondered how he could shuffle this duty onto someone else. He did not want to be around the infamous KiKu, let alone speak directly with him.

Obviously, no one else did, either.

He asked several officers, but they declined harshly, backing away from his annoying request.

Mustering his courage, Timon commandeered a pony cart with a servant holding a torch and trotted over to the dancing strobes of light from paper lanterns that signaled KiKu's rapid advance toward the Bhuttanian army.

While the regent empress was the most dangerous woman in the Empire, KiKu the Hetmaan was the most dangerous man in the Empire.

Timon hoped he would be able to recite the empress' message and leave.

One never knew with the renowned and loathsome KiKu.

One just never knew.

3

Maura sat at a table on a high dais.

Along with Rubank and the High Priestess of Magi, Maura sat upright, sipping colla tea Hasan Daegian style. She listened politely to poetry offered by a minstrel, but when the singer began reciting about love, the empress waved her off. She would rather hear about epic deeds of long-ago heroes.

Love poetry only made Maura feel sad. She had lost both of her loves, Dorak and Chaun Maaun, and would rather not be reminded.

The minstrel strummed on her lyre while singing a ribald song about a countess and her stable boy.

The Hasan Daegian women of Maura's court thought the song amusing, but their husbands found it demeaning.

The Hasan Daegian males had fought hard to win

legal and social rights. They finally had a matriarch who was sympathetic to their plight, and they disliked anything that detracted from their honors won fighting the last war, where they had made bold strides toward equality with women. The Hasan Daegian males studied the empress with interest.

Her eyes narrowed.

Many of the Hasan Daegian men turned their heads, so their wives could not see their smiles of relief at their ruler's displeasure. As Maura's eyes grew bright with anger, the men relaxed and leaned back in their chairs. Some even snickered at a particular verse. If the men hadn't had so much to lose, they might have thought the song was funny as well.

The minstrel, sensing the empress was not interested in her choice again, switched to peasant tunes she had learned from the Bhuttanians.

The Bhuttanians had no talent for art or music. Their songs tended to be uncomplicated, repetitive verses that demanded a call and response accompanied by a drum. But these songs would do until the minstrel could think of something else. As it turned out, she didn't have time.

The great gong sounded.

The minstrel was quickly escorted away.

The ancient Keeper Of The Palace waited for everyone to become quiet. It did not take long. "Great Mother," she boomed with her loud, steady voice. "Prince KiKu of Hittal asks permission to enter."

Maura nodded.

The High Priestess of Magi and Rubank rose to meet Prince KiKu, the famous spy who had helped topple the mighty Aga Zoar.

The Bhuttanians, after glancing at General Alexanee who gave a signal, also rose. They refrained from spitting on the spylord, who had betrayed their aga, though mutters and oaths were heard throughout the tent.

"I can't believe he would show his face here."

"I hope for his sake he doesn't sleep too soundly."

"May all his children see a painful death before his old age."

"He should be skinned alive."

"May his son sleep with his mother and his wife sleep with a borax."

Timon, who was sitting below the royal dais, could feel the electric charge in the air. He tucked his feet under his gown. For once, there was going to be excitement on this dreary march, and he was not going to miss it.

The High Priestess, overhearing some of the remarks, thought it folly for the empress to receive Prince KiKu publicly. Did the empress not realize the Bhuttanians hated KiKu, and their hatred of anyone always ran white-hot? She chanced a glance at Maura.

The face of the empress remained as impassive as carved stone.

The flap of the great tent opened. A tall, wiry man stepped forward into the smoke-filled pavilion of the empress.

Timon held his breath. Although he had delivered the empress' message, he had only seen a shadowy figure, who turned his face away. Timon was relieved that the spylord had taken no interest in him. The man had said nothing until Timon got the idea he should leave, which he did with haste. Timon scratched his chin in surprise. Now the great KiKu was before him, and he was as tall as any Bhuttanian.

Prince KiKu had harsh, black eyes, which darted quickly about. He sensed the hatred of the Bhuttanians. KiKu stifled a laugh. For years he had served the dreaded Zoar while watching his sister disintegrate under her marriage to him. Sweating and toiling under the hateful Bhuttanian yoke, KiKu was able to throw it off. Now he stood before the most powerful woman on Kaseri, who ruled over the despised Bhuttanians, his sworn enemies. It gave him great pleasure that she was not even Bhuttanian.

And the empress liked him—was even beholden to

him. No Bhuttanian dared touch him on pain of losing his head. KiKu chuckled to himself. This afforded him better security than having a hundred guards. Abject fear had its uses.

Followed by four women, KiKu strode toward the dais. His eyes fell upon some familiar faces. He remembered Rubank, a senior advisor to Maura's mother, Queen Abisola. KiKu was surprised at how Rubank had aged in the two years since he had last seen him. Recognizing the indigo robes of the High Priestess of Magi, he did not know the face. He would think about her later. Out of the corner of his eye, he spied General Alexance. He would have to watch that one carefully.

Finally, he looked upon Maura herself, feeling heat rising from her skin. It was like the sun's summer warmth.

The empress radiated a blue glow while emitting faint beams of gold and pink light from her hands and head. The power of the Mother Bogazkoy had not deserted her. The empress seemed a goddess. No wonder the Bhuttanians followed her.

KiKu breathed out slowly.

SHE MUST HAVE THE BOGAZKOY WITH HER!

The former hetmaan halted before the dais and knelt in keeping with Bhuttanian custom, folding his lush burgundy gown beneath him. "Greetings, Great Mother," he called out.

"Greetings, Prince KiKu of Hittal. Rise. I wish to see your face." Maura waved her fan impatiently while KiKu struggled to his feet. "I see you have acquired bad knees, Lord KiKu."

KiKu motioned to one of his companions to help him. "Old age, Great Mother."

"As well as too much rich food and wine," replied Maura, referring to KiKu's little potbelly.

Twitters arose among the court.

KiKu spoke quickly. "The gods have been good to me, Great Mother."

"What wind blows you here?"

"I have longed for the companionship of my empress and ruling lady. I wish only to bask in your infinite glory."

"As if there were any truth in those words, but never mind. May we be introduced?" the empress asked, pointing to the women standing behind KiKu.

"Great Mother, may I present my wives?"

Maura snapped open her fan, which meant approval in Hasan Daeg.

KiKu gestured to the oldest of the group.

A middle-aged woman stepped forward, looking frightened. Her eyes seemed to bolt everywhere, but one could sense a keen intelligence behind her plain face. The woman offered a silver box. Gently laying it on the first step of the dais, the woman spoke. "Great Mother, my name is Madric. I was taken prisoner seven years ago and sent to work as a tutor for a wealthy Camaroon in the Bhuttanian district of Zipei until I was liberated. I wish to present a token of gratitude for my release and reunion with my family." She stepped back.

One of the guards made her way to retrieve the box until the empress stopped her. "I'm sure it will give Madric great pleasure to open the box herself," purred Maura.

KiKu's face gave a faint impression of a smile. He had taught Maura well.

Death could be delivered in the guise of a gift by a friend. Madric stepped forward again and quickly gathered the silver box. With deft fingers, she undid a tiny silver clasp. "Great Mother, I present precious amber from my homeland."

She turned the box over, and large pieces of yellow amber tumbled onto the carpeted steps of the dais. "Purported to heal certain illnesses, amber can also be used in magic. It is my deepest hope that my humble gift will be acceptable to the woman who set me free from the terrible, dark place in which I had lived for so many years."

"It was not just I who has set you free, Madric," replied the empress. "Thousands have sacrificed so the yoke of tyranny could be thrown off."

The faces of the Bhuttanian officers grew dark at the implied insult to their former ruler but said nothing.

"Your gift will be accepted. I need earrings for my daughter. A small portion of this beautiful amber will do nicely."

Madric beamed at the suggestion that her amber would be used as jewelry for Princess Dyanna. She stepped back to her place behind KiKu.

KiKu motioned for another wife to approach the dais.

A woman in her late thirties with rough-looking hands offered a large leather bag. Opening it, she exposed hundreds of small vials filled with colored liquids. "My name is Pearl. I am a healer from the Qiowa river region. My specialty is fevers. I was taken five years ago from the city of Peygen and forced to work in Bhuttan. I first worked as a servant in the house of one of the officers who raided my home. A pox, unknown to me, overtook the city in which I had been placed. The wife and daughter of the officer to whom I belonged contracted the illness. I saved them, but the wife still sent me away as her husband began to love me. I then worked as a common laborer in the fields." She smiled briefly, revealing several missing teeth. "I escaped and made my way to Hittal where I met Prince KiKu. He honored me by marrying a poor one such as I."

Pointing to the vials, Pearl continued, "These are all the ointments and oils I use in the treatment of my patients. I give them to you to add to your medical knowledge." She handed a servant a scroll. "This is to be kept with the vials. It contains all the information needed to use them." Pearl bowed and returned to her place in KiKu's retinue.

The empress remained silent.

KiKu wondered if the empress was displeased with his wife's gift.

The empress spoke. "I am sure I speak on behalf of our learned physicians when I say your gift is most precious and generous. I thank you from the bottom of my heart."

Pearl's face lit up.

Though KiKu's face remained unreadable, he felt relieved. The gifts of his wives were accepted with much honor. KiKu was sure he had not lost favor with the empress. He motioned for the last two remaining wives. They were of similar stature and appearance.

The empress surmised they were sisters and the youngest of the wives.

They bowed graciously, and one could see they were suppressing giggles behind their pretty pink mouths.

The empress was slightly amused.

"I am Tippu," announced one of the girls. "This is my twin, Tippa. We are distant cousins of Prince KiKu. Most of our family died during the great famine. Prince KiKu found us and took us in. We are here to present you with a token of our esteem."

They laid down the heavy object they had been carrying and pulled off the shimmering cloth covering it. "We are artists, and we carved this out of obsidian."

The empress leaned forward to observe the statue. "May I ask the interpretation of this piece?"

Tippu's face flushed. "The woman in the carving represents you, Great Mother. At her breasts are two starving children suckling. The children represent— well," claimed Tippu, waving her hand at the congregation, "US!"

Maura had a servant bring the statue to her so she could touch it. "Again, I am delighted with a gift presented to me by the wives of an old comrade." She patted the statue. "I will take this with me all the way to Bhuttani, and place it in the official gardens of the aga's palace, where it will remain for the pleasure of all agas to come after me."

She turned to KiKu. "Thank you, Prince KiKu.

Couches have been prepared for you. Ask anything you need for your comfort, and it will be given to you."

Timon smiled as he watched KiKu being led away.

Not even the empress dared to incur the wrath of the Bhuttanian nobles by asking the traitor to dine on the dais with her.

Prince KiKu bowed, his face reflecting nothing of displeasure. KiKu followed a servant who made room for him near the Hasan Daegians and away from the hostile glares of the Bhuttanians. As he turned, KiKu met Timon's stare. His eyes, unsettled at the sight of Timon, did not betray recognition of the young scribe.

Timon gave a start and looked away. Composing himself quickly, Timon lifted his eyes to confront the infamous man, but KiKu was already escorting his wives to their couches.

Timon felt his heart pounding in his chest as he watched the former spylord approach his old comrades.

It did not go unnoticed by the Bhuttanians that all of the Hasan Daegians stood as KiKu had made his way toward them. To the Bhuttanians, he was a traitorous servant of their former aga.

To the Hasan Daegians, he was an honored servant of their people.

Such was the business of war.

Sooner or later, one of the Bhuttanians would kill

him, but not tonight with the Imperial Guards watching. The Bhuttanians turned their heads and resumed eating their meals. They were doubtful that KiKu would be alive for much longer.

4

The gangly scribe waited.

Timon stood with a little knot of impatient men wishing to petition the empress. He usually sat behind the empress, alongside Rubank, during court, but as the empress had invited him, he was to be treated as a guest. The wait gave Timon ample opportunity to study the proceedings without being noticed. Typically, all he saw was the back of the empress' head or the floor, as he could not directly gaze upon Maura. He missed all the subtleties of body movement and eye contact. And he was so busy translating for Rubank and waiting for the consul's responses, he missed the inflections of voice. He could now study the expressions and countenance of his betters.

He noted Maura cut an impressive figure sitting on her throne of bones, fixed on a rough-hewn dais covered with mats woven with intricate designs from Hasan Daeg.

Yellow flowers were interwoven into the braids of Maura's black-blue hair with its one lock of snow white at her widow's peak. Although her bearing was regal, Timon observed Maura's features to be average. She offered a severe expression with her blue-tinted eyes and their darker blue orbs, making her face resemble a mask. One could only guess what she truly thought.

Timon glanced about for KiKu. He was nowhere to be seen. The empress had not invited him to court. Timon tucked this information comfortably in his mind. He would retrieve it later when he could study the day's events in private.

On a lower level of the dais sat the High Priestess of the House of Magi with several other priestesses in their severe, dark blue-green robes. With their hands folded, they sat silent while their expressive eyes darted back and forth, surveying all things around them. Once in a great while, an older priestess dozed off for a few moments, but that was rare.

It was Timon's contention this was a ploy to put people off-guard. He was puzzled, as he could never discern the women's true purpose. They rarely advised the empress, and none of the information they collected was shared with the military or other advisors. They spent most of their time scribbling in huge books, cataloging everything they saw and heard on their journey to Bhuttan. He thought them a waste of the empire's money.

Behind the empress, on her right, was Rubank sitting with one leg on a small stool. He had problems with gout and had been placed on a strict diet by the royal physician. Rubank was the last of the older Hasan Daegian advisors who had survived the Great War, except for the fabled KiKu.

Surrounding this tight little group languished various military advisors and generals, both Hasan Daegian and Bhuttanian. They stood with their countrymen according to rank and did little to interact with each other.

The empress had forbidden fighting between Hasan Daegians and Bhuttanians, showing no partiality when sentencing to death those who disobeyed. So the former enemies had as little to do with each other as possible. They talked with their backs turned, chatting intimately among themselves reviewing the day's events.

Timon took in all of the little dramas of court. He found Rubank, as all Hasan Daegians, to be vain about his appearance.

The Hasan Daegians seemed an even-tempered people with occasional bouts of excitability when confronted with small, irritating matters such as a lack of clean water for baths. He thought their obsession with cleanliness to be ridiculous, though he had to admit the Hasan Daegians seemed to be sick less often than their Bhuttanian counterparts—and certainly smelled better.

Timon felt the hair on the back of his neck rise. He suddenly realized the empress was watching him observe the court. He forced his eyes up to the dais and met hers quickly. He salaamed by pressing his right palm against his forehead and lowered his eyes, but not before he saw her motion to one of her guards.

He waited obediently until the guard fetched him and brought him before the empress. Timon bowed very low, keeping his head pressed to the ground until the empress permitted him to look up.

"I see you are wearing a new robe, Master Timon," commented the empress, studying his tunic's fabric.

Timon blushed, not knowing how to reply. It embarrassed him that the empress took notice of what he wore. He could feel Rubank's worried eyes upon him and hoped he had not shamed his benefactor. It would only mean trouble for him later. Timon pointed to the detailed borax design embossed on the front of his robe, stammering, "Uh, this work is done by the women in my mother's village. They take great pride in their workmanship."

"Pray, tell me, where is your mother's village, good scribe?"

"My mother is from a remote village on the Plain of Moab. Less than four hundred people live there."

Maura leaned back and considered the young man standing before her. Tall and gaunt with spindly arms, Timon was anything but a soldier, only he was too young to realize it. She knew he dreamt of glory and chafed under his current position. Maura also knew he would be killed within minutes on the battlefield. Timon was so lacking the skills of a warrior that Maura could lean across the space that divided them and crush his throat with her bare hands before he realized what was happening to him.

The empress blinked and unclenched her hands. She motioned to a nearby servant, who spread out an old map. "Show me your homeland," she commanded Timon. "You may sit," she added as a servant brought a small stool.

The thin scribe blanched, leaning over the map. It was a detailed depiction of the known world drawn on animal parchment.

Timon's eyes followed the lines of the mountains to the rivers, which flowed near his home. He could not fathom why the empress would be interested in his tiny village. "It is here," he lied.

"Tell me about your homeland."

"What shall I tell you, Great Mother?"

"Anything. What did you do as a child? Do you love your mother? Who owns the spoons in the houses—the men or the women? Who is the most respected person in the village and why? Anything. Anything at all."

A thoughtful servant handed Timon a drink, and he took a sip while collecting his thoughts. "My people are nomadic. In the summer, we travel to the base of the mountains with our horses and grazing animals. There we live in small tents made of felt and leather. During the winter, we travel down to the steppes and live in houses made of stone." He looked at the empress.

She was quiet.

"Pray, continue," chimed in the High Priestess from the House of Magi.

When the empress did not stir, he continued. "I am the baby in my family with two elder sisters. I used to see them every summer when they came to the mountains. We do not speak of personal things, as it is not allowed between unmarried men and women. I do not know what the lives of my sisters have been like or how they feel."

"Very interesting," commented the High Priestess.

"What is, High Priestess?" Timon asked.

"The fact there is no personal conversation between

the sexes."

"As I have explained, we are a plain people. Our needs are few. There is not much to discuss besides the weather and our livestock." Timon twisted uneasily and added, "There is no need for us to talk. It only leads to trouble."

"How is that?" asked the High Priestess.

"Forbidden feelings. Taboo."

The High Priestess rebutted, "My young man, one does not need conversation for love, if that is what you are referring to. One only needs to behold another person. To connect in the eyes to connect in the heart." She studied him, trying to discern his age. She smiled thoughtfully. "You are too young to understand. Continue with other matters. How were you brought here?"

"When Zoar came through our region on his way to Hasan Daeg, I joined his army." Timon added quickly, "I worked with the horses until my superior noticed I had an aptitude for symbols and numbers." Timon sat up proudly upon his stool. "I have a way with words—written, of course—and I picked up the language easily once in Hasan Daeg."

"Zoar was searching for people who had a head for for symbols?" asked Maura, scowling at the bottom of an empty glass. It was immediately filled with colla tea.

"Yes, Great Mother. He was searching for these kinds of people. I was treated well and given lots to eat even though I trained many hours a day. I stayed in the ranks of the scribes until the royal consul sought me out and brought me thus."

"But you are not a true Bhuttanian," stated the empress, studying Timon's expression.

Timon's face grew red, and he blustered, "I am Bhuttanian, Great Mother!"

The Hasan Daegians noticed the Bhuttanians watched the royal party intently. The entire tent grew quiet except for the bustling noises the servants made.

The High Priestess said, "No offense was meant, Royal Scribe. The empress only meant to clarify the Moabites were absorbed by the Bhuttanian Empire before Aga Tnpothar's reign. According to oral history, the Moabites were a nomadic people akin to the Bhuttanians. They did not worship Bhuttu or Bhutta, but only one god who has no name. When the Moabites did not pay their annual tribute one spring, the Bhuttanians made war upon them. I make this comment because people of similar stock worship similar gods. Your people's god is much like that of the Anqarians—a god who is neither he nor she and has no name. It is only fodder for the mind."

Timon stiffened. He had made a terrible blunder

before the empress by expressing umbrage at her words. Timon's mind swirled with avenues of protocol to ease him out of this difficult situation, but he could not choose one. He slid off his stool and lowered himself before the empress, who studied him without expression. "Great Mother, please excuse my outburst! I spoke without thinking. You did not offend me. I am unused to being in such close proximity to your person in direct conversation. It caused me to be nervous and err like the peasant that I am."

"Rise, Timon. I take no issue with you. I wish to hear more of your country," replied the empress without rancor.

Alexanee, the highest-ranking Bhuttanian general, approached the royal dais. "Great Mother, may I speak upon this matter?"

Maura nodded, curious that Alexanee involved himself. She waved Timon back onto his stool and motioned with her fan for another one to be brought for the general.

Alexanee had a recent leg injury, which had not yet healed, and was grateful. "Great Mother, my mother's grandfather fought in the campaign to chastise the Moabites. There was only one great battle. As the Moabites were herdsmen, we quickly overtook them and placed our own man in their tent."

"Do you consider his people to be Bhuttanian?" asked the High Priestess.

"It is said the Moabites and the Bhuttanians were one people many years ago, but that overpopulation caused the tribe to split and go their separate ways. If we are not from the same fathers, then we are very close cousins." Alexanee turned toward Timon and pointed. "Notice the high cheekbones. The same ruddy, dark skin. He is a tall man like every Bhuttanian male." Alexanee grinned. "Not yet filled out, but he soon will be if the gods are kind."

The High Priestess spoke, "It is true these are hallmarks of Bhuttanian bloodlines."

The empress nodded thoughtfully and stroked the amulet around her neck.

Timon spied the amulet conspicuously, as did everyone when she touched it. It was rumored the necklace had belonged to the Black Cacodemon Zedek, who used it for his most powerful spells. Many whispered that the amulet produced magic from other worlds if one dared to use it.

"Tell me about your god," Maura commanded softly as she motioned for the musicians to play.

The musicians bowed and obliged by softly playing sad Hasan Daegian love songs.

The empress frowned at their selection.

The musicians quickly changed to a more upbeat tempo.

"It is just as I told you, Great Mother. Our god has no name."

"What powers does your god possess?"

Timon shrugged his shoulders. "One cannot say. Perhaps none, perhaps infinite."

"Where does your god live?" asked the empress.

"Legend has our god living in a lake on the steppes, but we have never seen it. It is only a rumor."

"Is your god male or female?" asked the High Priestess, rearranging her skirts.

Timon looked baffled. "I do not know." He paused for a moment. "I would say our god is neither, yet both."

"Did life begin with your god?" asked Maura.

"Yes, Great Mother."

Maura stated, "Then your god must be female."

"But one cannot deny that the spark of life begins with the male, Great Mother," pointed out the High Priestess.

Maura pondered for a moment. "Having a female goddess makes the most sense, but this boy says his god may be both."

"An oddity perhaps," murmured the High Priestess.

"No," said Timon, shaking his head. "It—he—she

is everything. We are part of it. We are one."

Maura straightened up, as did the High Priestess. The other priestesses began writing in their journals. "What did you say, Royal Scribe?"

Timon timidly looked at the tall and imposing empress sitting erect and stroking the huge uultepes lounging beside her with their eyes closed. "We are one."

"Why did you say that?"

"I—I don't know," stammered Timon. "It is something I have heard since my childhood."

"You have no priests or interpreters of your god, do you? No intermediaries?"

"Great Mother, we interpret for ourselves. We are one with this god; therefore, we listen to the god within us."

The empress leaned forward in her chair. "Tell me, Royal Scribe—and take care—do you feel your peoples' deaths without warning?"

One of the uultepes opened an eye and fixed it upon Timon, now squirming upon his stool.

"I feel sorry for anyone's death."

"No, no, no," scolded the empress, frustrated. "If a cousin of yours died, let's say, in a distant land, and you had no word, would you know she had died?"

Timon shook his head, seemingly confused at

the question.

Maura sighed and fell back into her chair. Ever since she had heard of the Moabites and their strange god who lived in a lake, she wanted to get close to a Moabite and learn all she could.

Timon would do.

She could see she was frightening the young man and decided she would let him retire from the dais to sit with the pretty girls who waited on the High Priestesses. Only Hasan Daegian male virgins and older widowed noblewomen waited on the empress. "You may go," she said, waving her hand in dismissal.

Wrung out, Timon was only too happy to escape the piercing glare of the empress. He bowed very low before the empress and salaamed gracefully.

Maura took no notice, as she was deep in thought. Suddenly feeling weary, the empress stood. Her uultepes immediately followed, yawning and stretching. One of them playfully swatted at the High Priestess.

She turned disdainfully, slapping the big cat on the end of its nose.

Maura did not reprimand her as the uultepes tended to rip, bite, eat, tear, or gnaw anything they could find. She did not blame the High Priestess for taking issue with her bodyguards. She did not even understand their presence, though she had called them forth from the

Mother Bogazkoy's secret chamber, guarding the remains of the beloved first Hasan Daegian queen, Rosalind.

Everyone rose to their feet. Bowing, they bid their empress good night. Though Maura had adopted many Bhuttanian customs, she did not like to sleep on couches in the middle of a tent with others, as had the former agas. She retired to her private chambers where a soothing bath and her lover for the evening awaited. The same person rarely entertained her twice, but mostly, she sent them away after questioning them about their lives. Tonight, though, she wanted to feel the pressure of hands on her flesh, have sweet words whispered into her ears, and enjoy cool lips on her neck. Maura entered her private bedchamber and smiled salaciously at the man who waited for her. Perched precariously on a chair, he appeared nervous.

She had chosen a Bhuttanian who had been a high-ranking official under her husband, Dorak. He was a tall and rough-looking man with several wide scars across his face. The Bhuttanian seemed jittery and at a loss for what to say. He asked Maura if her day had gone well.

Astonished, Maura regarded him. "Do you care if my day went well?"

The Bhuttanian shrugged his shoulders, not knowing what else to say. "I thought it might ease the strain if you talked about your day," he answered sincerely.

"Do you think I have tiresome days like other people? Like you, for instance?" she asked sarcastically.

"Of course, Great Mother," he replied, using the Hasan Daegian salutation. "You more than anyone." He paused for a moment. "Have I offended you, Great Mother? Perhaps I was at fault in comparing you to mere mortals?"

Maura went over to the Bhuttanian and stood before him. "Am I not like other mortals? What is the talk in the camp?"

Hesitating, the Bhuttanian finally peered into the empress' eyes. "They say you were once mortal, but you have mated with a devil tree, and now you are like one of the gods."

Maura gave a small laugh. She curtly dismissed her servants and poured her lover a cup of wine. Handing the cup to the man, she asked softly, "Does the fact that I may not be mortal frighten you?"

Happy that his hand did not shake, the lover revealed his tumultuous thoughts. Thinking he could not deceive her, he told the truth. "It frightens me very much, Great Lady. I do not know why you bothered to choose me. I am not young anymore." He shook his head in wonder and felt his face. "In fact, my countenance has little to admire. My wealth has been taken from me by misfortune. I have nothing to offer a queen, not even a gift such as a trinket."

"I think you have much to offer."

The Bhuttanian squared back his shoulders. "Though poor and broken, I will give what I can."

"Then I ask this of you. Make love to me as though I were a normal woman, one whom you desired." Maura felt the heat rise to her cheeks. "Can you do this for one night? I'll not ask more of you." She took the Bhuttanian's large, battered hands and pressed them to her breasts.

Realizing the empress might be lonely, the Bhuttanian took pity on her. "This I can do." He tried to hold her. "If only you will tell me how."

Seeing his stricken face, Maura laughed.

The Bhuttanian relaxed and laughed along with her.

She leaned forward, kissing him passionately.

He responded in kind and, picking her up, carried Maura to the bed.

"You will not find me ungrateful," Maura whispered. "In the morning, your property and more will be returned to you once you have pledged your loyalty to me."

The Bhuttanian lowered the empress on the soft bed. He was flushed with desire.

"I have one more request of you," said Maura.

"Ask, my lady, and if it is in my power, it is yours."

Maura looked deeply into his battered, questioning face. "Do not be gentle."

5

Maura climbed out of bed.

She donned nothing but Zedek's necklace. Touching the center of the amulet, she slipped behind her guards, going out the servant's entrance. Past dying fires and sleeping men, she sauntered unconcerned if one of them should awake. It mattered not for they would not be able to see her. She was invisible and would remain so for several minutes, the time needed to enter KiKu's chamber. She thought her entrance to KiKu's chamber easy until she saw the hetmaan sitting in a chair with only a small oil lamp casting a faint, warm glow about the tent.

KiKu gestured for Maura to approach when her unseen hand opened the flap to his private chambers.

Maura wrapped a blanket around herself and sat on a stool.

KiKu waited, seemingly undisturbed that an unseen force had entered his sleeping room. Finally, the spy could see faint features of Maura's face in the flickering of the oil lamp as she slowly became visible again. Her face was severe.

He waited for Maura to speak.

"Why are you here, KiKu?" she asked.

"I went back to my country, but there was no country to be found. The land was there, but my people had been scattered across the wastelands of Kaseri. Most of them are dead. The multitudes who have taken over my country are refugees from other places, and bitter ones at that. They have their own king and do not wish a Hittal to rule them. I have no army to force them." He paused.

"Is it my army you want?"

"For what purpose? To conquer a people who will always be in constant rebellion after your forces leave? I must face facts. They don't want me. They don't know the Hittal ways. It would be futile."

"Then why are you here amongst your deadliest enemies?"

He leaned toward Maura and whispered in her ear. "I have news that will interest you."

Dancing shadows thrown by the small oil lamp flickered across Maura's face.

KiKu thought her face was both cruel and beautiful, but it was her eyes, which spoke the most to him.

Maura could not hide the longing in her blue eyes. KiKu knew she wanted Dorak still. Not even death could spoil her love for him. "Speak! Speak before I lose all manner of patience with you," she hissed.

"The Dinii have been seen!"

Maura grabbed KiKu's arm and squeezed.

KiKu patted her hand while trying to coax her constricting fingers from around his pained flesh. "Maura, you are cutting off my blood," he said, using her personal name.

Maura immediately withdrew her hand. She lowered her head to her chest, trying to dispel the anguish rising from her bowels. "Tell me quickly," she begged.

"I have heard strange rumors from among the priests of Bhuttu. Strange bird-like creatures have appeared before several priests as apparitions begging for release at the great temple in Bhuttani."

"Release from what?" Maura pressed her hands together in agitation.

KiKu shrugged. "This is all I know, but I have been theorizing."

Maura looked at him in anticipation.

"What if the Dinii and Dorak did not leave the chamber of the Mother Bogazkoy of their own volition?" KiKu shifted in his seat and wrapped his cloak closer about him. "You told me that as you struck the death blow to the Black Cacodemon, you could not see what was happening on the other side of the cave."

"That's right," confirmed Maura.

"What if you didn't kill the bastard quickly enough? What if, between the first blow and the deathblow, he had time to utter one last incantation? He was still wearing the amulet you now possess. We do not know of all its powers. What if he willed the Dinii and Dorak away to a magical place, a realm of spirits?"

"KiKu, it would explain these horrible dreams I have been having since that terrible day."

"Dreams? You never spoke to anyone about dreams."

Maura smiled a twisted grin. "Do you have spies even in my tent?"

KiKu ignored her question, saying nothing.

Maura took it as a sign he did and congratulated herself on always assuming so. She continued, "I dream of Dorak crying out. I can barely see him except for his eyes, which are wide with fear. He calls to me, pleads for release from what I do not know. I see nothing, but I know he is in a dark and foreboding place." Tears, tinted blue by the gift of the Mother Bogazkoy, fell from her eyes. "I never accepted he was dead." She clutched at her blanket. "I never believed it."

"Make haste to the temple of Bhuttu. If the Dinii are seen, there must exist a portal from which they can return."

"Perhaps this is why they are being seen now. They can make contact, but cannot leave for some reason."

KiKu pointed to the heavy necklace around Maura's neck. "I would expect the amulet you possess is the missing piece. Take the necklace to the temple. If you must, torture the priests until they tell you its secret. Someone there must know something."

Maura looked thoughtful for a moment. "Or you could go."

KiKu shook his head sadly. "My spying days are over. Your balladeers have made my exploits too well known throughout the land," he claimed, not without pride. "I would be discovered."

"A former contact perhaps?" Maura asked, pressing him for commitment.

"All of the priests know each other well. They would not speak boldly before a stranger."

"How did you find out about the rumors then?"

"I cannot tell you without risking lives, but there are others besides the priests who have witnessed these phantoms."

Maura thought for a moment. "Perhaps we can train

someone for a special mission? Someone who is educated and well-versed in literature and religion." She turned to the tiring spylord. "Could you train a person for this mission?"

KiKu rubbed his sleepy eyes. "Yes, but not around here. I would have to take this person to a secluded spot and train him for several months. It could only be done with careful planning."

Extinguishing the small oil lamp, Maura prepared to leave. "You are tired, and I have much to think about."

The prince barely made out the young woman in the dark now. "Great Mother, there is something else I want to tell you."

"What?"

"An old friend awaits you in Bhuttani," he said.

Maura scoffed. "I have no friends in Bhuttani. Of whom do you speak?"

KiKu leaned forward, clasping Maura's mouth with his hand so she would not scream. Softly, he breathed, "Mikkotto!"

Also by
ABIGAIL KEAM

Princess Maura Tales

Josiah Reynolds Mysteries

Last Chance For Love Series

DEATH BY A HONEYBEE
A JOSIAH REYNOLDS MYSTERY
Book 1

Josiah Reynolds solves mysteries in the glamorous Bluegrass world of racehorses, bourbon, and antebellum mansions.

About The Author

Hello, my friend. I hope you are enjoying the Princess Maura Tales. I had such fun writing about Princess Maura and her adventures. If you like to read in other genres, I also write *The Josiah Reynolds Mystery Series* and *The Last Chance For Love Series*, a happily-ever-after sweet romance series. I would love to hear from you. abigailkeam@windstream.net

If you like my stories, please leave a review and tell your friends about me.

Visit me at **www.abigailkeam.com**